FROSTPROOF

FROSTPROOF

N.D. Ostroff

iUniverse, Inc.
New York Bloomington

FROSTPROOF

iUniverse books may be ordered through booksellers or by contacting:

iUniverse
1663 Liberty Drive
Bloomington, IN 47403
www.iuniverse.com
1-800-Authors (1-800-288-4677)

ISBN: 978-1-4502-5143-3 (pbk)
ISBN: 978-1-4502-5144-0 (ebk)

Printed in the United States of America
iUniverse rev. date: 8/3/10

Prologue

Recovery from the car accident was grueling; nasal feedings as my throat healed, the anguish of regular changes in gauze and packing on my arms and fingers, a constant morphine drip to keep the worst of the pain at bay.

Doctors told me I was lucky. Were it not for the sleet and wind cooling the burns my injuries would've been far worse.

I couldn't fathom worse.

Samantha's olive-colored eyes never lost their pools of devotion. She was there when I awoke from skin-graft surgery. She worked with me in rehab, helped massage my scarred fingers as I fought to grasp a pencil, encouraged me to tie my shoelaces when I wanted to quit. Seeing her face, her fawn-colored hair bunched over her shoulders, her glowing complexion, her warm smile, made everything almost seem okay.

But nothing was.

Our finances were in shambles. Samantha's waitress job and my former as a restaurant chef didn't offer health benefits. And the woman I'd tried to save didn't have car or life insurance.

By the time I'd gotten out of the hospital Samantha had sold most of our possessions to pay the mortgage. "For better or for worse, in sickness and in health," we'd proclaimed to each other last May. She had certainly kept up her end of the deal, clinging wistfully to ghosts of happier times.

I, on the other hand, have become a passionless replica of my former self. I've been unemployed since the accident, but not for lack of trying, my hands can no longer handle the intense labor and heat of working in a kitchen. And I've been depressed, drinking more than I should, more than ever before; spending our last dollars on booze. Some weeks the Seagrams whiskey and Budweiser bottles spill over the edge of our fifty-gallon recycling bin.

Samantha sobs at night in the bathroom before she comes to bed. She doesn't realize I can hear her. She thinks I'm drunk and passed out.

She doesn't know I'd risk everything to change our lives.

She's doesn't know I'd do the unimaginable.

Chapter 1

Somerset, Pennsylvania
Wednesday, April 22, 1:30 a.m.

Cody Larson was a big man, barrel-chested and full of prison-yard muscle and tattoos. We'd been traveling on the turnpike for several hours and were approaching the Appalachian Mountains when he told me to turn off at the next exit and head down a side road. He withdrew a small plastic bag stuffed with marijuana from his front pocket and displayed it in the neon glow of the dashboard lights.

"I got this shit off a college chick in Seattle," he said. "I figured we'd spark some here and then get back on the turnpike up the way."

He pulled out a sheet of crumpled aluminum foil, flattened it, rolled it into a tube, bent one end up, and molded it into a makeshift pipe. He dumped the marijuana into the bowl.

"Just like old times, huh?" he said.

I didn't acknowledge him. I was still thinking about the way I'd left home. The teary, disappointed expression on Samantha's face as I said goodbye and headed out. The lump in my gut that still remained.

Cody flicked his lighter and held the flame steadily over the bowl as he inhaled. Vegetative matter crackled and popped under the concentrated heat. He chortled and white balls of smoke rolled from his nostrils. A pungent, burning-hay odor suffused the interior.

He pushed the hot pipe into my hand.

"Take it!" he urged, his voice tight from holding in the draw.

He leaned his head back and blew out a stream of smoke that exploded against the ceiling and clouded the interior. He turned to me.

"What are you waiting for?" he asked. "Take a hit, buddy."

Something about the way he said the word *buddy* caused a shiver to run down my spine. As if we really were still pals. As if all the sleazy bullshit that had caused our friendship to all but vanish years ago had, in a strange way, vanished itself over the passage of time.

Coughing a bit, he added half-jokingly, "Don't make me force you."

I raised the aluminum foil to my lips, glanced at him and his stony grin, and breathed through the pipe. At first, I didn't even know if I was getting anything; the draw went down my throat smooth as ice cream. But then, fiery cinders hit the back of my tongue. I coughed through the mouthpiece causing tiny, flaming meteors to fly across the dashboard. I coughed uncontrollably, dropped the pipe, and lost my grip on the steering wheel. The car swerved, threw gravel along the embankment, and headed on a collision course for a pine grove.

"Look out!" Cody shouted.

I counter-turned, threw more gravel, fishtailed, and then got us back on the roadway. Cody snatched the pipe from between my feet and focused on igniting what still clung to the sides of the foil.

The car's interior came alive with revolving red and blue lights.

"Oh, shit!" Panic ricocheted through my brain. "Cops!"

A siren whirred and a police cruiser closed the distance between us. Cody lowered the pipe from his mouth; a sliver of smoke escaped his lips.

"What should I do?" I said, adrenaline-jacked.

"Pull over," he replied simply. "What else."

"What about Jake's arm? How are we going to explain that?"

Cody smiled crookedly and the corner of his mouth twitched. "I'll make certain they don't find the arm."

He leaned down and pushed the pipe under the floor mat, then lit a cigarette and dragged. I braked, edged to the side of the road, and parked. The cruiser quickly took up residence behind us. After a moment, an officer opened his door and stepped out. He put a hand to his sidearm and started toward my door. His partner stayed in the cruiser.

I rolled down the window as he approached.

"Evening," I said friendly-like, my stomach sick with worry.

"Shut off the car!" the officer ordered. "License and registration!"

I turned the key and the engine cut. A flashlight flicked on and the officer threw the beam into my eyes. I blinked at the sudden wash of illumination. The beam swung to the bits of scorched marijuana on the dashboard, to a drift of smoke hanging diagonally across the interior, and then into Cody's eyes. He squinted.

"Had quite a swerve back there," the officer said. "Anything you gentlemen would like to say before we proceed further?" He flung the light back into my eyes. "I'm assuming you'll give me permission to search the car? It'll make it easier on you both."

My heart chugged and I was almost certain the policeman could see it beating in the veins of my neck. I looked at Cody. He kept his face forward and his gaze ahead, drawing on his cigarette as if he were breathing through it; seemingly lost in his own world.

"You can't search the car," he said.

Another police cruiser pulled up with lights flashing. The officer beside my window signaled with a cautious wave. Two more officers opened their doors and got out. The officer beside my window stepped back, unholstered his weapon, and leveled it. My bladder suddenly felt very full.

He signaled the two other officers to take up positions behind my Sentra. They came around the back bumper. One leveled his gun while the other jotted down my license plate number.

"Both of you step out of the car!" the officer beside my window ordered. "Extinguish that cigarette and keep your hands where I can see them! Permission or no, I've got probable cause!"

Cody and I remained in our seats. My mouth went cotton-dry and my lips stuck together briefly as I opened them.

"What do we do?" I whispered.

The other officer stepped menacingly toward Cody's window.

"You boys deaf?" the officer said. "Exit the vehicle!"

I shifted in my seat and forced myself not to freak out. Cody clenched and unclenched his right hand. His face, silhouetted in the headlamps from the police cruiser, was dry except for a single drop of sweat that had rolled down between his eyes and now hung from the tip of his nose like a wart.

"Okay," Cody said, in a tone of finality; the corner of his mouth twitched. "I'm comin'."

I watched as he unhooked the keys from the ignition, opened the passenger's side door, and swiveled to step out.

"Get against the trunk!" the officer stated. "Hands where I can see them!"

Cody doddered around to the back and stood facing the car. Fear coursed through me as I moved to open my door.

"You," the officer said to me. "Throw the keys and get out!"

"I've got the keys," Cody said, and jingled them.

"Against the car!" an officer hollered at him. "Throw the keys and get against the car!"

"Whoops," Cody trilled.

He dropped the set. The officer closest to him looked down. In that brief instant, Cody launched himself into the man and pummeled him to the ground. They wrestled fiercely. The other officers lunged to help.

"Get his hands!" One of them shouted. "Oh Jesus, he's got my— "

Bam!

I jumped in the seat as blood spattered against the back window. The injured officer staggered up momentarily. There was a hole in his forehead where his right eye had blown out. Blood streamed down his face. He took a step and then crumpled to the asphalt.

Bam! Bam! Bam!

The officers fired. A bullet pierced the car door and whizzed inches from my side into the dashboard. Another shattered the rearview mirror.

Bam! Bam! Bam! Bam! Bam!

"Die! Die! Die!" Cody shouted, over the sound of repeated gunshots. "Die!"

"Officers down! Officers down!" the policeman in the patrol cruiser screamed into his radio's microphone.

Cody stormed toward the car and aimed his pistol. The officer fumbled for something and then raised his hands protectively and tried to duck.

Bam! Bam!

Two quarter-sized holes punctured the windshield. The officer slumped forward.

I couldn't believe what I was seeing. Feeling drained from my body. My cheeks went cold. I sat frozen in a complete state of shock, mesmerized with horror and disbelief, hands glued to the steering wheel, too numb to speak, too appalled to move.

An injured officer crawled toward the far cruiser. It was a sick movement, like a possum attempting to drag itself to the side of the road after being squashed by a tire. Blood poured from his side and colored his uniform with a spreading, crimson hue.

Cody advanced on the man and lowered the tip of his gun to the officer's forehead. The officer breathed fast and wept openly.

"Please, no!" the officer cried, his voice emptied of all brevity. "I have children!"

"And you're never gonna see 'em again!" Cody said. "Take a last look around at planet Earth, cop!"

I tried to scream, to holler *stop*! To shout. But I was so appalled I couldn't make a sound.

Bam!

The officer collapsed, legs askew, arms quivering.

Bam!

Another shot to the head. The ozone-metallic smell of gunpowder and fresh blood overspread the air.

"I like the way people look at death," Cody said. "Their faces are so gentle, so at peace. Every time I take someone out I feel as if I've done their soul a favor. Set them free in a way. And with it comes a high, know what I mean? The same high God must feel when he creates and destroys."

I felt woozy and breathed deep, filling my lungs with air, trying to comprehend and make sense of the moment.

"Jesus…What have you done?"

Totally unfazed by the atrocities, Cody calmly shook out a Camel cigarette from a pack in his back pocket.

"See how easy it is?" he said. "A gun is like a sorcerer's wand, complete control over life and death. Press the trigger and someone disappears. And they don't ever come back to bother you. Not ever."

My lips were numb and hard to control. My stomach lurched. "You've murdered these men. *Murdered* them!"

"Never liked cops much," He made a swiping gesture with his hand as if the men's souls had reincarnated into the mosquitoes now swarming around us and feeding from the corpses. "Power-hungry motherfuckers is what they are."

He leaned down, lifted his pant leg, and placed the pistol into an empty holster.

"Fits perfect! I'm glad they use .38's here in the East. I was beginnin' to feel uneasy without a piece. I lost the one that went in here somewhere around Indiana. Had a bit of a ruckus there."

Cody flicked his lighter and set fire to his cigarette. I should have done something. Maybe attacked him with the ice scraper or knocked him unconscious with the blunt spine of the owner's manual in the glove box. But I was scared out of my skin. Fear! Real fear! The kind that reduces even the largest horse of a man to a sobbing colt. And believe me, I was no horse. The complicated landscape of the human mind works in mysterious ways when faced with unanticipated, high-stress situations. My courage shut down completely. I sat in the driver's seat rabid with fear and intense hate for this man; but unable to act, unable to do anything, as he ransacked those dead men of their guns, ammunition, and supplies. He wrestled the jacket off the closest body and wiped our back window clean of blood. Then he loaded the materials into the trunk, got in, and dropped the keys onto my lap.

I wiped my lips with a trembling hand, realizing my whole world had irrevocably changed in an instant.

"Let's go," he said calmly.

I strained to control my outrage. "You're mad! I'm not going anywhere!"

"Normality, my friend, is defined by a person's level of emotional discomfort at committin' abnormal acts. I feel fine about what I did. Those men got in the way of what we've set out to do. What'd ya think would happen when they found Jake's arm? Didja think we'd talk our way out of it? Imagine what God would do if these guys harassed Him? I suspect the same thing."

"You're not God!"

His eyes squinted and seemed to sparkle in their sockets. "Not yet."

I dry-heaved and swallowed repeatedly.

"I'm going home!"

"You'll do no such thing!"

A car drove up. Its lone occupant stared out the window with wide, horrified eyes, and then quickly pulled around us and accelerated.

"Murder!" I exclaimed. My whole body shook. "Fucking murder! These are human beings spread in front of us! Police officers for Christ's sake!"

"Speakin' of which," Cody interjected. "We'd better get outta here. Cops'll be swarmin' this place in minutes."

Lingering effects of the harsh hit of marijuana whipped my thoughts into a paranoid frenzy. I envisioned myself hauled off to jail. I imagined Samantha staring at me through the protective glass at the maximum security visitor's room, tears streaking down her face asking; *Why? Why? Why?* And me sitting in handcuffs trying to explain that I had nothing to do with these crimes, nothing at all… and no one believing me.

"I'm not going any further!" I made a feeble effort to straighten my posture. "I'll drop you at a bus station or train station or wherever you want! You can have the money! You can have everything! I'll keep my mouth shut about what you did, but I'm not continuing!"

"We made a pact." Cody's jaw muscles bunched. He grit his teeth and spoke with a low, heavy growl. "Let's go."

"I… I can't!"

"You will!"

"No!"

He pushed a gun into my hand. "You've only got one out! Kill me! Put a bullet through my brain! Go ahead. No one will be the wiser. You can drive this piece-of-shit car back to your piece-of-shit life and the money and smack will sit there, year after year after year, rottin' in the ground, same as the regret that will rot inside you, turnin' your guts black. You could've been rich. Could've kept that beautiful wife and home. Your morals, buddy, not my actions, will ruin your life."

I shrunk back from him. "Murder in cold blood! I can't accept!"

"Killin' is an instinctive act that lies outside the realm of culture's principles. The situation needed resolution. The cops were gonna search the car. They would've opened the trunk and found the arm. Didja want to spend the next twenty years rottin' in a jail cell? Cause that's what woulda' happened to you as an accomplice to Jake Romano, which you and I would be labeled. This was self-preservation." He paused. "So what's it gonna be? You takin' my life or do we continue with our treasure hunt?"

The gun slipped from my fingers and clattered against the center console. I glanced in the rearview mirror. Grisly red rivers flowed from the three bodies sprawled on the blacktop. Larger and more aggressive night insects had arrived for the morbid feast.

I cranked the engine and slammed my foot on the gas pedal. We took off, tires squealing. Surrounding nightscape smeared into a blur of shadow and dappled moonlight. Odors of burned rubber filtered through the vents.

"Give me a drink!" I stated. "Give me that bottle!"

Cody reached behind him into my bag and pulled out the Seagrams whiskey. I spun the cap and swallowed greedily, grimacing as the liquid drained down my throat. I tried to steady myself. Tried to rationalize what had just occurred.

"Take it easy on that shit," Cody warned.

"Fuck you!"

I kept my eyes focused out the windshield because I couldn't look at him; at his face, so at ease with what he'd done.

"Had no choice but to resolve the crisis this way," he spoke. "My way. My terms. Survival of the fittest is what it's all about. What's four fewer people takin' up space anyway? Consider me the ultimate human population controller."

My hand trembled as I gave the bottle back to him.

Cody stowed the bottle under his seat. "My actions are deemed immoral by a culture only if it violates their rules of the moment. During a war, my carnage against the enemy would be acceptable, even encouraged. This is a war we're wagin'. To the victors go the spoils. You'd better get that through your head."

He pulled up his right pant leg and withdrew a Phillips head screwdriver tied to his calf with an orange bandanna. He used the tip to scrape off tiny red drops dried on the back of his hand.

"Didja know a screwdriver is one of the most versatile weapons in the world? Think of the injury it can do to the human body when properly executed."

I suppressed the urge to pull over, throw open the door, and run; run like the wind. Take a chance on racing into the wilderness and escaping this madman. But Samantha flashed into my mind. And then the policeman's blasted face. And the maroon, almost blackish color of his blood. And the officer crawling for his life. And Cody smiling as he pumped another round into the already dead officer's forehead. And what Cody could do to Samantha if he took revenge on me for leaving.

Cody stuck his hand into his back pocket and came out with the map. He unfolded it, dabbed his index finger into a large drop of not-quite-coagulated-policeman-blood pooled in the fold of his t-shirt, and traced an unsteady line from Philadelphia, Pennsylvania all the way across the paper to Seattle, Washington.

"Don'tcha worry 'bout nothin'," he said, and patted my shoulder with his other hand. "I'll take care of anymore problems."

I clenched at a sudden sharp pain in my belly, slammed on the brakes, threw open the door, and vomited.

Chapter 2

Coal Town, Pennsylvania
Wednesday, April 22, 4:25 a.m.

We traveled in silence for a long stretch. Numb with shock, so stunned I could hardly think straight, I tried to untangle the impossible knot Cody's violence had tied in my head. Portraits of horror hung in my mind.

I couldn't believe that I had agreed to this trip. I couldn't believe I was caught up in this madness. I couldn't believe I had been so stupid as to have invited Cody into my home.

Marks in the palm looked like cuts in raw chicken; an X, a mangled triangle, a cross sliced into the fleshy part at the base of the thumb. Fingers had curled into a grotesque claw and bluish mold grew around the fingernails. Where the splintered radius and ulna bone should have met was a blackish stump. A fetid odor of spoiled meat drifted off it.

Cody raked his hand through his mountain of dark hair. The colorful cobra tattooed along the side of his neck seemed almost alive. I hadn't seen or heard from him in years but I knew he'd grown up in a house with a pill-popping mother and an abusive, alcoholic father. I'd always believed that upbringing caused his strange behavior and eccentricities in college. But this was a human arm! The real thing! Right in front of me!

"A map?" I questioned.

"Bingo!"

I handed Cody the arm and drank from my nearly empty can of Budweiser. The sight of the arm knotted my stomach.

"Benny Harvin is the only other person alive who knows what I'm about to tell ya," Cody said. "And the only reason he knows is because he's involved."

Benny had lived four doors down the dorm hallway from us junior year. He was a moose of a man with curly blond hair and a round, dumpling face, and would do everything from steal your beer and cigarettes, to try and date-rape your drunk girlfriend. He was the biggest sleaze I'd ever met.

"I thought Benny ratted on you?" I said. "That you hated him?"

"I do."

"Then why— "

"Niles!" Samantha's voice fired down from the top stair. "Is someone in the basement with you?"

Cody whisked the severed arm behind him and almost knocked over his beer. I glanced toward the steps suddenly realizing that I'd forgotten to inform my wife that while she was in the shower the man who had once led me down a dark road populated by criminals and drug dealers and nearly destroyed my life, had shown up unannounced after ten years.

"My old college roommate, Cody is here," I replied.

I waited to see if she'd overheard our conversation or noticed the arm. If she'd come stomping down here screaming, "Why is this criminal in my house!"

"Hello, Mrs. Goodman," Cody called up.

"Oh, hello," she said, and the door slammed shut.

"Remember Jake Romano?" Cody continued unfazed. "The heroin dealer from off-campus?"

The vague image of a tall, spaghetti-thin man with bad acne and a missing front tooth popped into my head. "Yeah."

"About a week ago, he planned to buy a huge stash of Peruvian smack from this guy, who it turns out, was with the FBI. Jake discovers this, kills the guy, and steals the heroin. Panicked, Jake grabbed his cash from the last fourteen months of deals, all recently laundered into crisp, untraceable hundreds, and drove to the Seattle suburbs to hide the stuff. That fucker was so freaked out over what he'd done that he got doped up out of his skull on the way. Not wanting to forget where he buried the stash, and not having a writing implement, he carved these marks into his own skin to remind him."

I felt queasy.

"On his way back, he gets into this wild shootout with the cops, and gets hit, but eventually makes his way to his apartment. That's when Benny contacted me. Jake didn't last long after I got there. Died right on the kitchen floor. So we stuffed him into Benny's Dodge and drove off to Puget Sound to dump the body. And wouldn't ya know it, we didn't have

nothin' to copy the map with. All we had was a knife. So we cut off the arm. Here we are covered in Jake's blood, carryin' his arm, and the police are scourin' the city. We knew we couldn't go back to the apartment, at least not with the arm, so Benny and I made a pact. I'd take it and leave Seattle, and he'd keep an eye on the whereabouts of the law. This way neither of us could get the money without the other's help. He needs the map and I need to know when it's safe to return."

"I'll get you a pen and paper," I said. "Get rid of the arm."

"Copying the map won't do any good. Benny wants to see the real McCoy. He don't trust a duplicate."

Cody stood, stretched, and tucked the arm back into the green army duffle bag he'd brought with him. The stench that puffed out when he opened the drawstring nearly knocked me over.

"Benny's given me the all-clear to return," he said. "That's why I'm here. I want you to come along."

I almost laughed and would have had I not seen his expression; steely and devoid of humor.

"You're serious?" I said. "Drive with you to Seattle?"

"There's $800,000 and about a million worth of stolen Peruvian smack buried in the dirt. If we work together, I'll split the cash. That's four hundred grand tax-free." He tied the drawstrings shut. "Big incentive to take a road trip, aye buddy? Money is the ultimate panacea."

I realized my jaw was hanging open and closed it.

"What about Benny?" I asked.

Cody looked at me steadily. "Who deserves the money more? An old friend? Or the fucker who swindled me into prison?"

I drained the last of my Budweiser. "Let me think about it."

"What's to think about? Do ya wanna be rich or not?" He withdrew a pack of Camels and offered it to me. "Want one?"

I shook my head. "I quit. Been chewing Nicorette nicotine gum for months."

He pulled a cigarette. "Mind if I do?"

I shook my head again, not really thinking about the question.

I got up and paced the length of the basement; passed books, old clothes, and boxes of Samantha's paints and canvases. I was crazy even to consider this. Traveling with Cody? I must've been out of my mind.

Cody reached into his front pocket and withdrew a girl's neon-green sports watch. Drops of dried blood partially obscured its clear plastic face.

"4:25 a.m.," he said. "We've made pretty good— " He paused and cocked his head. "Hear that?"

Air screamed with the distant wail of sirens. Cody jerked around in his seat and squinted to see in the dim arc of morning.

"Cut the lights!" he ordered.

My blood went cold.

"Cut the fuckin' lights!"

I did as he said and slowed down.

"They can't be after us!" I stated. "We're two hundred miles away!"

The clamor of noise grew louder as it grew closer.

"Whatever the ruckus, we're gonna be dealin' with it soon enough," Cody said, and his mouth twitched. "Unless… "

He aimed a finger at a cluster of shoulder-high foliage about a hundred yards off the road. "Pull behind those."

"That won't hide us!"

"Do it! It's still dark enough! The cops' attention is focused forward! They ain't lookin' to the side!"

I wiped sweat from my forehead with a badly trembling hand.

"I can't do this!" I stated. "I can't run from what you've done!"

"You will!" Cody looked at me with dark-as-death eyes. "This'll work! Pull the car into those bushes!"

He gripped my shoulder. "Do it!"

Every inch of my skin prickled with terror. Several squad cars appeared in the far distance as a line of flashing reds and blues. I pulled off the road, eased into the brush, and avoided the brakes. I opened the door. The interior light blinked on.

Cody's hand flew up and shattered it. Blood spurted from a gash in his palm.

"We've gotta cover the reflectors so their headlights don't catch!" he stated.

He jumped out and ran around to the trunk. I followed.

"Get the left side!" he stated.

Fighting panic, I bent over the bumper using my body as cover. We remained like this eyes glued to the oncoming patrol cars. My whole world heightened to a feverish pitch. Before we knew it they were upon us and we stood in the fringes of their headlights. I held my breath as each car passed in a roar of dust and exhaust. The noise was like a wind.

Whoosh!

Whoosh!

Whoosh!

Whoosh!

Within a few terrifying seconds that felt like an eternity, they were gone and off into the morning. Coos of waking birds and sporadic chirps of retiring crickets enhanced the new calm.

"Told you it'd work," Cody said. He spat. "The cops'll think we're travelin' so they'll focus their search ahead of us. We'll stay here until there's more traffic on the road and then blend into it for cover. Cops'll be three states away by the time they figure out they're chasin' phantoms."

Adrenaline coursed through my veins. I ran around to the front of the car, threw open the driver's side door, and reached frantically for the Seagrams. I spun the cap and guzzled in choked gulps. Nausea panged my gut.

"Easy on that stuff," Cody said.

I felt the alcohol warm my blood and numb our reality. The image of Samantha's face became a beam of light left sifting through the darkness collecting inside my head.

"Niles?"

"Huh?" I grunted, and opened my eyes.

Slowly, the real world effused. I lifted my head from the table. At first, I couldn't make sense of the bizarre shapes and blurred objects. Then I closed my left eye and squinted with the right. I was in the kitchen. Samantha stood beside me with her arms folded. She cast a bitter eye over the half-empty Seagrams bottle and the line of spent beer cans.

"You're drunk!"

I scratched my cheek, gradually coming more awake. Alcohol-induced pain poked at my brain. I groped around for some response but my voice stuck in my throat. I leaned my head back and stared at the ceiling. The room began to tailspin.

"I'm sorry," I said.

"You always apologize after the fact!" she exclaimed. She inhaled and let the breath out sharply. "Niles, I've told you a thousand times that I hate the drinking! I'm not going to try and change you! You have to want to change! If you're going to drink your life away then you're going to do it alone!"

My heartbeat pounded in my head.

"And worse," she continued. "You've invited someone like Cody Larson into our home. He's been sitting in the living room since— "

"The living room?"

I'd completely forgotten about my former friend's presence. I stood fast. Flocks of bright dots sparkled across my sight. My legs went rubbery and nearly let out. I reached for the back of the chair for support.

She scowled. "You need to get control of yourself! No more drinking today!"

I nodded. "No more... I promise."

She left the kitchen and headed down the hallway. I stood a moment, recalling my previous conversation with

Cody. A golden opportunity had presented itself. A chance to pay off our debts. A chance at riches. A chance to give Samantha the life she deserved. I couldn't shake the thought of having that much money from my mind. What it could do for us.

Of course, the adventure had risks. The crime of possessing the detached arm of a cop-killing drug lord, for one. Not to mention the million bucks worth of heroin we'd be carrying by the end of the journey.

I thought long and hard. Felt alcohol dulling my reasoning process.

Risk vs. riches? The answer came the way a shooting star brightens the dark gulf of the night sky. I had to go.

I took a wobbly step, and when my legs held me steady, took another, and staggered into the living room. Cody was slouched on the canvas chair staring with a blank expression at the television as he watched a voiceless Pat Sajak flicker on the screen. Oliver, my Beagle-Spaniel mix was sprawled on the floor with his snout on his forepaws.

The tick, tick, tick, *of the wall clock was the only sound.*

"Seven-thirty already," I said, squinting at the clock and trying my best to appear sober. "Guess I lost track of time."

"I've been waitin' patiently for an answer," Cody said, and turned in my direction. "But my patience is about spent. Have ya decided? Are ya in?"

I moved beside him, lowered my voice, and nodded. "Yes, I'm in."

He looked at me steadily; his eyes deeply sunken and laced with tiny red veins.

"Good." He pushed up from the chair and gestured toward the front door. "Let's go!"

"Now? I can't just up and go at the drop of a hat. I need time to get my things together. We'll leave in the morning. You can spend the night in— "

"No! We gotta move! Time ain't a luxury we can afford. Not yet."

"Is the money going somewhere?"

"It ain't the money I'm worried about," he replied. "I don't know how well Jake wrapped the smack and I can't, I won't, take a chance on it spoilin' in the Seattle rain!"

The idea of junkies sticking needles with contaminated heroin into their arms and then collapsing like dominoes in the wet reflective streets turned me cold inside. Cody smiled, drew close, and draped his arm around my shoulders. The onion stench emitting from his pits was nearly eye-watering.

"We're talkin' about enough cash for you to buy the wife practically anythin' her little heart desires," he cooed. "Enough cash to change your lives forever. But we gotta go now."

I shifted uncomfortably and backed away from his hold.

"Okay," I said. "But give me an hour at least. I need an hour."

"You got one, but that's it. You okay to drive?"

My stomach still spun, but with each passing moment I felt slightly more like myself. "I'll be fine."

Cody withdrew a cigarette and swaggered toward the front door. He took a fast look into the kitchen and halted in the entranceway. "Got any aluminum foil?"

"Second cabinet, first shelf. Why?"

He grinned. "I got a treat guaranteed to make ya feel like a college kid again."

Chapter 3

New Castle, Pennsylvania
Wednesday, April 22, 6:45 a.m.

Minutes passed.

Ten.

Fifteen.

Twenty.

Cars sped down the highway like mechanical ants following a scent trail. Overhead, clouds had raftered together and blotted out the sun.

"You okay?" Cody asked.

"You're a monster," I replied.

He smirked. "Monster is an interesting word. Do you think a blue jay is a monster because it kills other birds that nest in its territory? How about a whale that murders millions of Krill in a single mouthful? I'm no more a monster than a housecat who snuffs out a mouse. Or a tiger that takes down a gazelle. Killin' is a tool necessary for survival in society. No, buddy, I'm not a monster. I'm enlightened! Top of the food chain!"

"You murdered those men! They're not a food source!"

Cody squinted. "They're food for worms."

He spun his head and looked out the back window. "Traffic's clear! Let's get outta here!"

I started the car, unsnapped the emergency brake, rolled backward out of the shrubbery, shifted into drive, and gunned it up to the road. Air had turned moist and leaden.

We drove in silence for a couple miles and eventually merged with the flow of vehicles.

Suddenly, traffic slowed and then nearly stopped altogether. Horns blared. The line of stationary gridlock reached over the hill toward the horizon. I looked around for a way out; a side road or a turnoff. There was none. A feeling of doom sunk over my shoulders.

"Must be a somethin' up ahead," Cody said. He fished the map from his back pocket. "If I remember correctly there's a fire road bypass around here. It's rugged, but should take us over the Allegheny Mountains. We can rejoin the interstate in Ohio."

"What if you're wrong?"

He sparked a cigarette. "Then the frostproof will have to come into play."

"The what?"

He didn't reply. Just kept on smoking steadily.

* * *

Traffic stirred. We maneuvered slowly through the lanes, and eventually, to my tremendous relief, turned off the highway onto a swath of cleared vegetation that looked more like an old bike trail then a road. Wheel ruts were deep and rocky, with high, dry grass growing between them. A few vehicles tried to follow our lead but quickly backed up and turned around. They must have thought we were crazy to continue on such a desolate route.

The car bottomed out and tossed our heads against the roof.

"Easy," Cody said. "This road'll tear your car apart. Take it slow."

"You sure this'll get us to the highway?" I asked. "Cause we're down to a quarter tank of gas."

"A quarter tank will get us there," Cody replied. "It merges just over this next ridge."

The tires hit another deep pit. Mud sprayed onto the side windows.

"Careful!" he shouted. "Watch the road!"

I gripped the steering wheel. The car started to shimmy and a low, steady thump emitted from the left side of the wheel well.

"Shit!" he said. "That don't sound good."

I stopped the car and poked my head out the window. Dread fell heavy.

"The tire's flat," I said, and tried to keep my voice even.

"I figured that," Cody replied. "Let's get the spare. And hurry. We gotta make up for this lost time."

I looked away afraid to meet his eye. A few yards down the roadway a crow landed, pecked at some carrion, and then flew off.

"There isn't one," I said.

An unsettling grimace came over his face. "I didn't just hear that."

"Samantha ran over a nail last week and we couldn't afford a replacement tire. So I put the spare from this car onto hers."

He got out of the Sentra and stepped around to examine the damage.

In a sudden burst of fury, he kicked the driver's side door and dented the metal. He kicked it again, and again, spewing his anger in bursts. He leaned inside the window, across me, and rummaged through the ashtray. He withdrew a mashed cigarette butt, lit it, huffed two drags, and then threw the remainder onto the ground.

I opened the door and slowly got out of the car.

"What do we do now?" I asked.

The whine of a siren made us both jump. I whirled my head around and saw a cloud of dust coming our way. Ahead of the dust was a police cruiser. Cody leaned down, pretended to scratch his leg, and unhooked the .38. He stood upright, stretched, and discreetly tucked the weapon into the back waistband of his pants.

The cruiser pulled up and stopped beside us. An officer rolled down the window and hung a meaty arm on the rim. The officer's quiescent features were bloated and his gray hair sparse. In fact, he looked remarkably like Boss Hog from the 1970's television show *The Dukes of Hazard.* Had I not been so petrified I might have even chuckled at the uncanny resemblance.

"Car trouble?" the officer asked.

"You could say that," Cody replied. "Tire's flat."

"I wouldn't doubt it," the officer said, with suspicion in his tone. "This road is for municipal vehicles only. What's a coupla' guys like you doing way out here, anyway?"

Cody flashed him a disarming smile. "We were just tryin' to make up for lost time. Got caught in a traffic jam a ways back and we stumbled onto this. Didn't know it was off-limits."

"Didn't know, huh?" The officer clamped his fingers underneath the window frame and pulled his mass from the cruiser. "You…" he said to me. "Where're you coming from?"

Fear caused my tongue to feel oversized and I could hardly say the words I'd spoken a thousand times before. "Chalfont County. About thirty miles outside of Philadelphia."

The officer stepped a little closer. He appeared tense. He looked down at our misshapen tire, the damaged right side, and the bullet-smashed side mirror. He eyeballed Cody's T-shirt, streaked with threads of dried blood, and unsnapped his holster.

"You boys turn around and put your hands on the hood," the officer said.

"We haven't done anything wrong!" Cody protested, and stepped toward the door.

The officer's hand drew to his gun. "Stop!"

Cody froze. His eyes narrowed into slits. "I was going to get the registration."

"Keep your hands in view! I'll deal with that in a moment. Get against the hood! You boys stay like that while I call this in. If you ain't done nothing wrong then you'll be on your way shortly."

"Unit 453," the cruiser's radio squawked. "Copy."

The officer turned his head toward his squad car. Cody jumped forward, whipped his leg up, and roundhouse kicked the officer in the face. The officer pinwheeled backward. His hands flailed and reached for the open squad car door. He missed and toppled to the ground. Cody ran up and dug the muzzle of his own .38 into the officer's glistening forehead.

"Don't!" I screamed.

I lunged at him, and then stopped when I caught sight of the demented look on his face.

"Let's go!" I stated. "Cuff him to the car! Let's get out of here!"

Cody turned his head slowly and looked at me with craziness in his eyes. "We've got a flat, remember?"

Cody turned back and looked into the officer's horrified face. The cruiser's radio crackled white noise

"Unit 453, copy," the radio called. "This is Lieutenant Wayne McGovern of the Pennsylvania State Police. Respond, copy."

"Answer that!" Cody ordered. "Tell 'em everythin's fine!"

The officer remained a sprawled statue of fright.

"Move!" Cody yelled. "I ain't foolin'!"

Cody kept the pistol level as the officer shuffled to his knees, crawled toward the radio, and then took the microphone in his hand. His jaw opened and seemed to lock up.

"Unit 453, copy!" the radio squawked more urgently.

"Speak!" Cody ordered. "Answer them or die!"

The officer slowly depressed the mic.

"C-copy," the officer stuttered. "Th-th- this is unit f-four-five-three."

"Unit 453," the radio responded. "I'm supervising the case of the Harrisburg homicides. The suspects may be entering your district at this time. All units in the surrounding counties are on high alert for suspicious vehicles, copy."

Tense moments passed. Eyes flashed to faces. Faces flashed to the radio.

"Unit 453, respond. Copy."

"Say somethin'!" Cody ordered, and waggled the gun. The side of his mouth twitched. "Say something now!"

The officer made a writhing grimace.

"I'm not fuckin' around!" Cody stated. "You have three seconds to answer! One… " He paused. "Two… "

He pushed the muzzle hard against the officer's forehead. Sweat flowed from the officer's face and blended with the blood leaking from his broken nose. His left eye had ballooned shut.

"Copy!" the officer uttered in a terrorized squawk. "Th-this… " The officer's Adam's apple jerked up and down as he spoke. "…is unit 453. P-please advise. C-copy."

"453, we've alerted all units in your vicinity to this crisis and who we believe the suspects are. We've compared prints from a homicide in Seattle, Washington and a double murder in Tiffin, Ohio and one in Billings, Indiana. They all point to a fugitive named Cody Larson, who escaped from the Washington State Department of Corrections Psychiatric Wing several weeks ago. Use caution should you encounter the fugitive. Larson is in an extremely violent and psychotic state of mind. We believe Larson is traveling with someone. The suspect or suspects may be armed and are certainly dangerous. Copy."

I stood by my car, my mind reeling. The bloodshed, the brutality, the killing, the madness; it all began to make sense. Cody was insane.

The officer's eyes bugged out in sudden terror as Cody took a step backward and aimed the .38.

"No!" I shouted.

"Oh, Jesus!" the officer screamed, and lifted an arm to protect his face. "Help me! Oh Christ!"

An explosive crack, like a baseball player hitting a line drive, echoed through the air. A finger flew off the officer's hand and a small, black-rimmed hole appeared in his head, followed by a syrupy stream of blood. The officer fell over; a sack of bones.

All the strength left my body. My stomach clenched. My legs gave out and I slid down along the side of the Sentra to sit in the mud. I started to cry.

Cody squatted beside the officer, felt his wrist for a pulse, then let the hand drop. He stood, stepped back, and fired another round into the officer's chest, at the heart. The corpse jittered from the impact.

"Now he's dead," Cody affirmed, and raised his eyes to me. "I don't think I'm in an extremely violent and psychotic state of mind, do you?"

"Unit 453! Unit 453, copy! Copy! 45— "

Cody switched off the radio. Tears streamed down my face. Nausea twisted my gut. I felt myself slipping into a shocked faint.

"Oh, get over it," Cody said. He reached into the cruiser and pulled the communications radio from its housing. "Whadaya think he was gonna do? Let two guys with a battered, bullet-riddled car drivin' around the back roads of western PA go on their way after that report? I just saved you from a lifetime in prison. My actions will allow you to see your lovely wife and home again. So, a 'thank you' at this point seems mildly appropriate instead of the 'I hate you' scowl that's on your face."

The curtain of my mind drew closed.

"I said a 'thank you' would be appropriate, don't you think?" His voice got louder. "I said, don't you think? Goddammit give me some appreciation!"

I didn't want to look at him, at his face, so at ease with this slaughter.

"Hey, thanks a lot!" I spat. "Thanks for getting me involved!"

"Don't mention it," he replied, in sudden, good-natured reproof. He held up a 12-gauge shotgun he'd taken from the rack bolted to the cruiser's back window. "This is the kind of power I like, a large-scale damage inflictor. Even this guy's sidearm is an old-style Colt .45. It'll put a hole the size of a golf ball in ya. Wonder why this backwoods boy scout carries so much firepower?"

"Probably to use against killers like you," I muttered.

"Ya think?" Cody came toward me in such a rush my heart fluttered. "What're the odds that he'd actually face someone like me? A human more intelligent, more enlightened; a superior animal! Talk about not being prepared. Talk about being caught off-guard. Stupid ass deserves everything I— "

"Shut up!"

He glared at me.

"The guy's dead!" I shouted. "You killed him!" I looked down at my hands and wept openly. "You fucking killed him, Jesus Christ!"

"Okay, Florence Night'ngale, we'll leave it alone." Cody crouched next to the cruiser, his attention now focused on the tire. "We gotta work fast. That MacNamera character has probably sent notice to dispatch that there hasn't been a response."

My hands and legs trembled. I got up and reached into the Sentra's glove compartment for a piece of Nicorette. Cody took the keys off the dead officer and opened the cruiser's trunk.

"Dammit!" I exclaimed.

"What?"

My gaze slid uneasily to the blood oozing from the officer's head.

"It's nothing," I said.

"Yeah, I chewed your gum. I'm outta smokes."

Cody pulled the jack and the lug wrench and started work changing the tire. He rigged the cruiser's oversized rim onto the Sentra's brake assembly and pounded it in with his fist.

"We'll stop at the first market we see and get you some gum and me a few packs, okay?" he said. "The tire's ready, let's go."

He sounded as if we were kids on a summer outing in need of supplies.

* * *

We stopped after a dozen back road miles. Cody hopped out, sprung the trunk, put the police radio between the front seats and ran a wire to the battery. A red light popped on and the device crackled to life.

"Now we'll know what's going on with the cops," he said, and flicked the dial until we heard police chatter. "We'll stay one step ahead."

I didn't reply, just stared ahead through the dull afternoon sunlight.

Chapter 4

Somewhere in Ohio
Wednesday, April 22, 4:15 p.m.

We merged back onto the highway, crossed the Ohio River, and then turned north toward Lake Erie. We filled the gas tank at a convenience store, bought smokes for Cody, and then turned back off the highway and continued through isolated country roads. Roads with no streetlights or houses. The store didn't carry nicotine gum.

Thanks to the information provided by the police radio, we avoided checkpoints set ahead of us and traveled hundreds of miles without further incident. I had begun to believe the worst of this nightmare might be over. But I also believed our use of the police radio would turn out to be our biggest mistake if we continued to rely on its information. The cops knew we had it and would eventually use it to trap us. But I didn't say anything about my worries to Cody. He wanted the device on and I wanted to avoid confrontation.

"Turn here," Cody said. They were his first words in hours. "There's a lodge up ahead that caters to people like us. We can chow and rest for an hour. You look like you need it."

"I don't want to stop," I said. "I just want to get there. I'm not tired."

"I think we should stop and rest!" he said adamantly, and pointed to a large, dark, shadow of a building up ahead. "Stop the car!"

"I don't want— "

"Stop the fuckin' car!"

I braked and skidded to a halt in front of a warped sign entwined in vines and hanging lopsided from a rusted metal post. *Creekside Inn* ran along the length of the wood. Ahead, massive tangles of weeds grew around a huge, dilapidated barn-like structure badly in need of maintenance and paint. Tree branches gnarled the roof in hideous ways.

"You'd better start listening to me," Cody said. "Or things ain't gonna go well."

He opened the door, stepped out, put his hands to the small of his back, and cracked his spine.

"Smell that mountain air," he said, looking completely at ease. "That'll rejuvenate ya. Come on buddy, let's go snare some grub."

"I don't want to snare grub! I want to keep moving!"

"Nonsense!" Cody jerked a thumb over his shoulder. "C'mon."

"No!"

He glared at me. "Get out of the car!"

I sat defiant. "What are you going to do if I don't?"

He sighed. "Just get out of the car and take an hour to enjoy yourself. It's so much better than the alternative."

I hesitated, and then did as he said.

He seemed to know his way through the shoddiness and I followed him around a rusted wrought-iron fence, crossed a mildewed plank over an algae-infested creek, and then stepped onto a splintered porch. He opened the unlocked front door without knocking and we stepped inside a pleasantly cool and spacious room, like a converted stable.

A faint, slightly unpleasant, fruit-gone-sour aroma lingered in the air. Wood walls danced with the orange glow from a dozen burning candles and petroleum lamps. A stuffed moose head and elk head leered from above a charred stone fireplace. Three tables set with newspaper as placemats and tarnished silverware took up space in one corner. And in the other, an old, dusty jukebox sat unplugged beside an empty cigarette machine with cracked front glass.

A willowy young woman with a spray of freckles emerged nearly soundlessly from a side door. Hair the color of ripe strawberries hung to her waist. Her eyes, even in the low-lit atmosphere, gleamed hazel. She wore a yellow housedress that accentuated petite breasts, a tight abdomen, and athlete's legs.

"Hi, guys." She smiled as if she'd been expecting us and flashed Cody a glance wrought with familiar overtones. "You here for a meal or rooms?"

"Both." Cody turned to me. "Hungry?"

At the mention of the word I suddenly came aware of the emptiness in my belly and the heaviness of my body. Though I had disagreed with him about stopping, we were here so I may as well accept. It still took effort to nod.

"You boys sit where you want," she said, and grinned at me. "My name's Kara. I'll be right back with menus."

She curtsied and then quickly dismissed herself.

Perhaps the stress, or lack of sleep, or the fact that I'd witnessed numerous murders over the last few hours, was making me paranoid; but I suddenly felt acutely wary of this woman and watched her intently as she left the room.

* * *

Kara returned a few minutes later with two slips of torn notebook paper scribbled with four items. The spelling of the items was atrocious. I couldn't even make out what they were.

"It's so nice to have people," she said. "Papa was going to convert the guest rooms to storage space but I insisted we leave a few open." Her eyes ranged up and down the length of me. "Just in case a couple of cute travelers happen to stop by."

Cody smirked, trying his hardest not to bust out laughing.

She touched my arm and then bent over to light the candle in the center of the table. Her breasts brushed against my shoulder. I noticed pink scars running in horizontal lines along her wrists.

"Would you guys like some water?" she asked. "I have lots of bottles of water. Lots of bottles."

"Do you have any alcoholic beverages?" I asked.

I sensed the burn of Cody's disapproving stare.

"Alcohol?" She looked blankly over my shoulder into space. "I... uh, don't know. I have lots of bottles of water. Papa might have some alcohol in the cabinets. I have lots of bottles of water in the cabinets, too."

She scurried from the room.

"Careful, buddy," Cody warned. "A drunk soldier is worthless in battle."

My head pounded with the hate I felt toward him for putting me in this situation; the hate I harbored for sacrificing my future to save a stranger in a car accident; the hate for being poor and not providing to my wife.

"Fuck you!" I stated. "Fuck you! Fuck you! Fuck you! If I want a drink I'm gonna damn well have one! Nobody... especially you, are going to tell me otherwise!"

Cody opened his mouth to reply but Kara entered the room.

"We have Budweiser beer," she said cordially. "That has alcohol in it."

Cody chewed on his lower lip and kept his gaze on me.

"That's fine," I said.

"And what would you like to eat?"

"Gimme a steak and make it bloody rare!" Cody said, still eyeing me. "Real bloody!"

Kara nodded. "We have eggs this evening." She turned to me. "And what would you like to have?"

"I'll have a beer and.... " I looked down at the illegible notebook paper and then back at Cody. Unimaginable stress had transformed my empty stomach into an acidic cesspool and I couldn't think of anything except drinking a beer and filling the gnawing, growling space with food. "Eggs."

"Okay," she chirped, and added a quick little giggle. "I'll be right back with your selections."

She took the pieces of paper and left out the side door.

"Quite a hot piece of ass, ain't she?" Cody said. "What do ya think?"

"About what?" I asked.

"Her."

"What about her?"

"What a great fuck she'd be."

"I'm married."

Kara returned. "Papa said you can have two rooms for two hours for twenty dollars. How's that sound?"

"We won't need that long," Cody replied. "We'll be outta here in an hour. How about ten for the two rooms for one hour?" He smiled wickedly. "And maybe I'll throw in a tip."

Kara nodded and placed a beer and a glass of water in front of me, and a glass of water in front of Cody. Small pieces of dirt floated in the water.

"After you eat I'll show you to your rooms," Kara said. "I'll be right back."

I found myself actually salivating as I raised the beer can, popped the top, and upended it. My stomach clenched as the room temperature liquid hit my taste buds. I gagged and sprayed the mouthful back into the can and onto the table. Dry-heaving, I wiped my lips with the newspaper.

"That's the worst thing I've ever tasted!" I exclaimed. I picked some of the particles from the water and rinsed my mouth. "What the hell's going on around here?"

Cody sipped his water and picked a hair out from between his teeth. "You think she gets an electric bill? Or a telephone bill? Or even mail? We're in non-existence here, buddy. What she's got is what we get. That's how it works. This ain't a place too many people know about."

I clasped my head in my hands. "What have you gotten me into?"

Cody opened a packet of sugar and dumped the contents into his mouth. He washed it down with more water.

"There's no turnin' back, ya hear? We're in motion and we ain't stoppin' until that money and smack is in my hands." He moved his fingers into the shape of a gun and placed it against his temple. "There's only one way out and you ain't got the guts."

I raised my glass of water, tried my best to conceal my quivering hand, and sipped. My stomach felt so tight I wasn't sure if I could keep the liquid down, let alone eat.

Cody leaned forward, and in the low, flickering light of the candles and petroleum lamps, with his shaggy black hair accenting hydrocephalic features, his face assumed the guise of a demon. His cobra tattoo looked alive.

"In a coupla days this'll all be over for ya," he said. "And you'll have reaped the reward of a lifetime."

Something about the way he said those words caused the skin on the back of my neck to prickle.

* * *

Unusual and pungent odors wafted from the kitchen. A few minutes later, Kara strolled into the room carrying two plates piled with watery, yellow mounds. Cody whispered something into her ear as she placed the plates before us. She left and returned with more packets of sugar.

We ate the meal despite the food's foul odor and taste. When we finished, Cody got up from the table and went about finding a cigarette. He strode in a few minutes later chewing the filter of an unlighted one and carrying a battered pack of Marlboros. Kara followed.

"Come on," he said. "She'll take us to our rooms. We got thirty minutes to relax."

I got up slowly, feeling numb from exhaustion and sick from the sour taste of the eggs. Kara led us down a long hallway illuminated by shimmering candles. Stale air reeked of mold and something long ago rotted. We approached a pair of door knobs caked in dust. Lacy cobwebs bunched in the doorframes.

"This room is for you," she said to Cody.

She pointed to the other door and leaned into me.

"And this one's for you," she whispered, and her lips brushed against my ear.

Heat rushed to my face.

"Uh... thanks," I said. "Thanks a lot."

She flashed me a sexy look of vulnerability and then slinked away.

"She likes you," Cody said, with a smirk. "I'm goin' out to the car to get my stuff. I'll be right back."

I turned the knob and pushed open the door. Hinges squeaked. Unlit, half-burned white candles lined high, rectangular walls. The bed, an old Victorian style with a thick wood frame, was dressed with a white sheet blotched with yellow, off-color stains. An old three-drawer dresser was beside an empty closet.

I went to the window and watched Cody retrieve his duffel bag. I followed after him into his room, which looked pretty much the same as mine.

"Close the door," he said, and unfastened the top.

Stronger, more sinister odors encompassed the room. He lifted Jake's arm. The flesh had turned willowy and pale, tinged here and there with daubs of dried pus. The fingers had shriveled and curled into a spidery fist.

I thought how unusual the arm looked without the attached torso. How the skin appeared like wax when there were no cells bustling in microcosmic activity.

Cody put the arm on top of the dresser. He pulled out and uncapped a bottle of rubbing alcohol, spilled it over some rags, and wiped the arm down.

"We should get rid of that," I said. "We don't need the added risk."

He dribbled more alcohol over the fingers and forced them apart so he could disinfect between them.

"I already toldja, it's our proof to Benny. End of discussion!"

"Proof for what? Christ, you've known Benny long enough. What's he think you're gonna do?"

Cody raised his eyes. They were dark-ringed and bloodshot.

"He thinks I'm gonna cheat him out of his take. And I am. But not the way he thinks."

Cody wrapped the arm in the alcohol-soaked rags, stuffed it back into the duffel bag, and fastened the top.

"Benny doesn't trust anyone and neither do I," he continued. "'Cept for you, of course. Anyone could easily fake a map to nothin' and then collect everythin' later."

He broke thought, stared dazedly for a moment, and then added; "I have a paper copy in case the arm rots away. We just need to show him the arm."

* * *

I sat on the side of the bed too wired from the horror of everything to rest. A light tap sounded at my door. My heart kicked up.

Another soft knock.

"Come in," I said.

The door opened slowly and Kara's thin shadow stretched across the wood floor. Her head poked through the space.

"Am I disturbing you?" she asked, and stepped into the room.

She had changed clothes and now wore a white oxford shirt unbuttoned to expose her cleavage and a brown miniskirt. The style looked like something from the 1950's.

"Papa said it's okay if I come to your room and spend some time with you," she said.

"Excuse me?" I replied, not grasping the meaning.

She crossed to the bed and glided up to me. "Papa said it's okay. Papa and Cody talked."

Her hands took mine and she pulled me silently into the hallway. I don't know why I went. Perhaps, it was the same reason I was still with Cody. Fear if I resisted. We stepped past Cody's open door. He was sitting up in the bed smoking a cigarette and staring absently at an empty spot on the wall. He didn't acknowledge us.

Kara led me passed two more doors before reaching one that had a shiny knob and wood polished like new. She put her index finger to her lips.

"Shhh. This is Papa's room."

"Why are we going in here?"

"Papa wants to meet you."

She pushed open the door. Smells of mildew and rot doubled in my nostrils. The room was similar to the rest, except with a little less dust and relatively few cobwebs. Objects looked as if they hadn't been touched in years. She stepped inside and candlelight from the hallway overspread the bed. Atop the neatly dressed mattress lay a figure covered from head to toe in sheets browned with age.

Something white reflected in the light.

Bone?

I hardly had time to realize what was happening when wet lips pressed against mine. The intensity of Kara's mouth, her tongue, surprised me. I gagged and tried to disentangle. She hooked her fingernails into my shoulder blades and ripped open my skin.

"Stop!" I hollered, and pushed her away.

She pulled down her miniskirt. A forest of pubic hair grew between her legs.

"Fuck me!" she seethed. "Fuck me!"

The same eyes that had been wide and innocent in the restaurant suddenly clouded with hate.

"Get out!" she shrieked. "You've woken Papa! Get out! Get out!"

She burst into tears. I raced out of the room and into Cody's.

"What's wrong with you?" he asked gingerly.

"We're leaving!" I stated. "She's crazy! This whole fucking place is crazy!"

Cody ran his fingers through his hair. "Did she take you to Papa's room?"

"The guy's a mummy! A mummy!"

Kara entered the room murmuring; "I know what to do, Papa, I know what to do, Papa. I know what to do, Papa."

Her face contorted. She let out a sudden, ear-piercing scream and vaulted at me with a butcher's knife flailing in her hand. Cody jumped up with an armful of blanket and tackled her as she passed. The knife clattered to the floor.

"I'll kill you!" she screeched, as she went down. "Kill you!"

She struggled fiercely against Cody's grip. "How dare you wake papa! How dare you! I'll kill you!"

"Shhh... relax sweetheart, relax," Cody cooed.

He wrestled her into submission and kissed her forehead. She went limp, as if he'd flicked off a switch in her mind. He turned to me, winked, and then turned back to her.

"I left the money in the jar as always," he said. "We're gonna go now, okay?"

She nodded mutely, her face pallid and timid-looking again. Cody released his grip. Kara curled into a fetal position and began sucking on her thumb.

"She'll be like that for hours," Cody said. He stood, brushed himself off, pulled the neon green girl's sports watch from his pocket, and checked the time. "She's somethin', huh? I thought you might like her."

I stared at him incredulously; weak-kneed, sweating, feeling like someone had inserted needles into my abdomen.

"You set this up?" I said. "She's a hooker."

"That's right, and don't be so goddamn righteous about it. One of Kara's little side enterprises is givin' the best fucks this side of the mountain. Truth is, I wanted you to have a little fun."

"Fun? You bastard! You're trying to turn me into something I'm not! Keep your sleazy lifestyle away from me!"

He grabbed his bag and swung the weight of it over his right shoulder. His eyes narrowed.

"It's time we head out," he said. "I'm gonna throw this in the trunk. Meet me in the kitchen in five minutes. We'll grab supplies."

I looked at Kara lying on the floor in a near catatonic state of bliss, and almost retched.

* * *

Cans of vegetables breaded in dust, discarded propane tanks, food so moldy it formed giant green mounds on the warped wood countertop, an old-fashioned deep-sink overflowing with ancient, food encrusted dishes; this was the kitchen at Creekside Inn.

A cockroach skirted passed as I reached for a partial six-pack of Budweiser coated with a layer of grime so thick I could hardly read the labels.

"Ready?" Cody asked, startling me as he entered.

He shook out a Marlboro Light and snapped off the filter. The cigarette was so old the paper had turned brown.

"Look at this place," I said. "We'll be lucky if we don't get food poisoning. God knows what kind of animal those eggs were from."

He shrugged, ignited the cigarette, and coughed out smoke.

We walked outside. The sun had dipped behind the curvature of the Earth and the puffy clouds from earlier had flattened into brushed orange streaks. Air was fragrant with the aroma of honeysuckle and mountain flowers. If it weren't for the fact that we were heading into the unknown, and the corpses of five people were behind us, and police from a dozen counties were hunting for us, and I'd just spent the last hour in the company of a sexual psychopath, I'd have said it was a beautiful evening.

Cody made a quick check of his reflection in the passenger side window.

"I'll drive?" he said. "I'm in the mood."

I nodded mutely.

He sauntered around, opened the driver's side door, and folded into the seat. I glanced once more at the Creekside Inn and dropped into the passenger's seat. Cody flicked on the police radio, took out the map, and traced with his index finger just outside the line of blood.

"It won't be long now," he said.

We pulled out of the grassy space and continued our journey down the desolate country road.

Chapter 5

Mansfield, Ohio
Wednesday, April 22, 8:45 p.m.

We located a gas station in a small town and filled the tank. The attendant shot odd glances at our out-of-state license plate and the damage to the car, but we were off before anything came of it.

For the first few miles out of town the stretch of highway was lit under the spectral glare of streetlights, but as we turned onto a deep wilderness back road, we plunged into darkness. I stared at the black clumps of trees whizzing passed and listened to the static from the police radio.

Exhaustion weighed on my body.

I remembered reading stories of soldiers so weary from battle that they would drift off to sleep in the middle of a firefight even as bullets slapped dirt inches from their positions.

Many never woke up.

That's what kept me from closing my eyes.

I was surprised at the clarity of my head now that my mind had drained of all inebriating substances. For the first time since before my car accident injuries and hospital stay my thoughts came sharp and clear, without the lingering fog of painkillers and booze. Enduring the long road to recovery; each day, hazy, filled with hurt, and drifting into the next, took a heavy toll on my optimism. I realized the damage my depression and self-abuse had done to my life and my marriage, turning me from an ambitious young newlywed into a bitter, apathetic shell of my former self. In my current state of sobriety, I realized I had to change.

Now, staring out the car window, traveling with a psychotic killer beside me, in my clean state of mind, the horror of the car accident came back to me, and the good deed that had changed my life forever.

The world was a white winter storm. Driving on the Pennsylvania Turnpike toward Doylestown, the minivan ahead of me started to fishtail. It veered out of control, skidded over the center lane, and rammed into the median, then ricocheted across the icy road and careened into a telephone pole. The pole snapped, crushed the roof, and blew out the windows.

I stomped my brake pedal and skidded to a stop. I quickly dialed 911.

"There's been an accident!" I stated. "On the PA Turnpike, about four miles north from the Doyle— "

Orange flame ignited under the hood.

"There's a fire! The car's on fire!"

I dropped my cell phone, scrambled from my car, and sloshed toward the wreck. The front section of the minivan was compressed into a pile of mangled metal. Steam poured from the almost nonexistent radiator and flowed over the ruptured hood. Green antifreeze spilled onto the snow.

A young woman groaned. The steering column had buckled and impaled her body against the vinyl seat. Her forehead was bruised and deformed from impacting the windshield. Crumbs of safety glass stuck in her cheeks. Blood ran from the bridge of her nose to her chin.

Her eyes roved slowly toward me.

"Ja… cob," she moaned. "Ja… cob."

In the smashed backseat I saw an infant strapped to a carrier. The infant was conscious but silent. It looked uninjured. Flames around the engine licked higher.

I tried to open the door, but it was too bent.

Odors of gasoline drifted into my nostrils. Fire burst through the minivan's rear windows and wrapped around the vehicle. A brilliant orange explosion lit the sky and blew me back several feet. Thick smoke huffed upward.

"Jacob!" The woman shrieked and thrashed in the seat. "Jacob!"

Adrenaline-jacked, I lurched to the flaming wreckage and pushed my hands through the shattered back window. The sleeves on my chef's coat ignited. Hair on my arms, face, and head incinerated. I caught hold of the baby carrier, pulled with all my might, and stumbled backward.

Next thing I realized I'm on my back getting tapped with pellets of sleet. I looked down. Jacob's body was blistered and lifeless; the baby seat slightly melted around him.

I left Jacob's remains in the roadway and floundered toward the barreling heat and fire. Orange light danced across the frozen landscape.

Not thinking, I reached out with both hands and grabbed the driver's side door handle. My fingertips dissolved against the hot metal with a sizzling hiss. I howled and inhaled a lungful of superheated smoke.

I stumbled backward hacking and spitting into my raw palms. I banged into the Sentra and slid down its side. Vapors of smoke skirted above what remained of my scorched chef's coat. My checkered polyester pants stuck wetly to my legs. My throat was a tube of hurt.

I dipped my hands into the snow and sat in profound sadness. Wind flowed across the highway and fed the flames. Precipitation changed into quarter-size snowflakes. My teeth chattered from cold and shock.

Blurred lights and the crunching sound of an oncoming vehicle proceeding through the foul weather meant nothing.

I wasn't thinking about help as I watched the woman burn.

I was thinking about how much I loved Samantha.

"You okay?"

In the absence of light, Cody was a voice, nothing else.

I straightened my spine.

"Why dontcha get some sleep?" he said. "Go on. I'll wake you if anythin' happens. We've got the trust thing goin', right?"

"The trust thing, huh?" I said. "You don't have any trust with me! You do what you want no matter what I say. You don't tell me anything of what's happening."

"What are you gettin' at?"

"What's really going to happen when we reach Seattle? How's Benny going to react when he has to give me all that cash?"

Cody flicked off the police radio and kept his eyes straight ahead. "We're meetin' Benny in Seattle because he knows the same people Jake knew. People who will buy the heroin. But that's where our relationship ends! He ain't gettin' any of the stashed money. Not when we've been takin' all the chances, riskin' our skins to get the arm back while his fat ass is planted safe in his apartment watchin' *I Love Lucy* repeats."

"How did Benny meet up with Jake in the first place?" I asked.

"It's a long story that happened a long time ago." Cody's voice flowed steady and mean but the emotion wasn't directed at me. "Back in college, Benny was makin' tons of coke and heroin buys, stealin' money from the guys in the dorm to buy quantity, then divvyin' it out and sellin' dime bags to the locals at the bars. He knew I dealt with Jake and begged me to introduce him, promising me over and over that he wouldn't compete with the people I sold to. His buyers were a small group of steady users, he said. No complications."

Cody twisted the filter off a cigarette, lit the tobacco, and dragged.

"Fat fuck took my buyers so fast I had to deal with people I didn't know just to stay in the scene. That's how I got set up. In fact, I got reason to believe Benny and Jake pushed that narc on me." Cody glanced in the rearview mirror. "Now it's payback time."

I rested my elbow on the window frame and put my chin in the palm of my hand. "If you hate Benny so much why are we meeting him at all?"

"Benny associates with people who can afford to buy the amount of smack that's out there. I need him to verify to the dealer that I've returned and then set up a meeting. Ideally, I'd like to unload the shit all at once."

"What about the cash?"

"Once I've got the junk and I've been introduced to the buyer…" His voice went menacingly low. "I'm gonna kill the motherfucker."

Our conversation ended abruptly as he flipped on the car radio and blasted *The Doors, Break on Through to the Other Side.*

"I love this fuckin' song!" he shouted, and banged his hand on the dashboard to the beat. "Break on through... Break on through... Break on through to the other side. Oh yeah!"

* * *

Talking with Cody passed the time. Nevertheless, it was an uneasy trade-off. The more he talked, the more I listened, and the more I began to understand him, which was not a good thing at all.

Chapter 6

Gary, Indiana
Thursday, April 23, 7:20 a.m.

Morning arrived, gray and cheerless, cold for late April, and windy. Heavy traffic, low gas, and hunger finally forced us to brave civilization and seek supplies. Cody drove off the back roads and onto the highway. He pulled into a marina parking lot along the southern tip of Lake Michigan, braked, took the keys from the ignition, and got out. His long hair blew in a black storm above his head.

My legs were cramped, my butt felt like an iron plate, and I smelled as if I'd just run a marathon. I opened the door, unfolded, and stretched. Wind slapped waves against the concrete breakwater and blew bits of sand against my face. Seagulls arced overhead. Silhouetted against the stratosphere, a jet cruised east. I imagined myself on that jet, returning home with bags of cash, my problems magically gone along with the nightmare of this trip.

"I'm starvin'," Cody said, jarring me back to the immediate.

He circled my Sentra. "You go to that country store we passed and get some food while I hunt for another ride. This one's had it."

"What are you talking about?"

He stepped closer. Dark pouches sagged beneath the cartography of his vein-laced eyes.

"Your car. It's time to get rid of it. Time for something new."

He withdrew his last cigarette, tore off the filter, and crumpled the pack.

"We're not getting rid of my car!" I stated.

"I'm gonna need smokes, too," he added.

"Did you hear me?"

He stepped and closed the gap between us. "Do as I say! Understand?"

I glared at him, resenting his sudden cauldron of authority. He dug a twenty-dollar bill from his pocket and held it out to me. There were spots of blood on the paper.

"I'm gonna go do what I do best," he said. "You do what I tell you and everything'll work out fine." He pulled up another twenty. "Get more of that cigarette gum if you want."

My desire to smoke had evaporated like my desire to drink.

Cody did an about face and strode away. I stood in a daze with absolutely nowhere to turn for help. A desperate man caught up in an unimaginable situation… with no way out.

* * *

I'd never felt more in love with Samantha and the dismal little life I'd created for us than at that moment. If a genie could've granted me three wishes, the first would be that Cody never came into my life, but the remaining two I would give to my wife, for she more than anyone, deserved to have her wishes come true.

I popped a piece of Nicorette and headed upstairs. The drinks I'd consumed earlier had almost completely worn off and left me with a shaky, disconnected feel.

I entered the bedroom. A laundry basket of clothes was on the bed. Samantha had been folding, but now stood in a daze, staring at a blank point on the wall. She looked at me and her face crumpled.

"We're in trouble," she said, and struggled not to cry. "That was the bank on the phone. They want the past due mortgage checks by the end of the month or… " She dabbed at the corners of her eyes with a sock. "Or that's it. They're going to foreclose. We'll lose everything."

Bile bubbled from my stomach and burned the back of my throat. I reached into my pocket for a Tums, only to find an empty wrapper.

"What did you tell them?" I asked.

"What do you think? I said we'd have it by the thirtieth. We can't lose this house, Niles! If we lose this house we've got nothing!"

My toes clenched inside my shoes.

"I've been thinking about it," she said. "If I sell my car we can probably go another month. I can sell some jewelry, too. That might give us another month after that. And then your car... "

Something inside me shut down. All I could think about was the bottle of Seagrams stowed in the kitchen cabinet; how it could make my problems disappear. I followed Samantha's gaze to my hand and realized I was scratching my arm, scratching at the patches of scar tissue.

"I can get the money," I said, and cleared my throat. "There is a way."

She looked at me with an almost comical expression of doubt. "How?"

I hesitated and toed the carpet. "Cody."

She pursed her lips. "Excuse me?"

"Cody needs someone to work for him. For about a week. We'll be taking my car."

She threw down the sock. "Are you insane? You're not working with that criminal!"

I forced myself to keep looking at her. "I already agreed."

"You what?" She stood with hands on her hips, her chin jutting out. "No way! I'd rather lose the house!"

"But, Sam— "

"No buts! No explanations! You're not getting involved with him! The guy spent years in jail! That experience changes people! Prison changes people!"

"Keep your voice low. He's right downstairs."

"I don't care! He's screwing with your head, Niles! He's screwing with your rational thinking! He's a violent drug

dealer! You once told me you think he killed a guy! How could you even entertain the idea of working for him?"

"You don't understand."

"I don't want to understand! Why is this scheme any different? He talked you into dealing drugs in college and almost got you busted! He had you stash his gun in your apartment while the police searched his! He once even asked you to smuggle cigarettes to him while he was on trial! He's always been trouble!"

"This is different. We'll be traveling most of the time."

"How is that different?"

My sight raked the room and searched for something to focus on other than her angry face.

"You need to find real work," she said, and her voice caught in her throat. "All you've done lately is drain our liquor cabinet."

I scratched at my scars and looked out the window. The sun crested the horizon and threw reddish brilliance across the sky. Birds were settling for the night.

Samantha sighed. "I know these last few months have been tough for you... for us. But going away to work for Cody? Listen to how crazy that sounds! Whatever his scheme, whatever his motives, it's going to turn out bad. We both know it. We've got enough problems without his intrusion and dirty charity. I'd rather be living with my mother than have you spend time with him."

Silence ensued. I thought about what would happen a month from now when the mortgage was due, again. I thought about what we'd have to sell next to survive. I thought about what would happen once there was nothing left to sell.

"I have to go," I said. "It's the only way."

She picked up the laundry basket and held it under her arm. "I've dealt with your rehab! Your therapy! Your recovery! I've done everything I know to keep this marriage alive." She shook her head. "All those times I came home exhausted from busting my ass at the restaurant and then went to the hospital to sleep in that lumpy guest chair so I could be with you when you woke up. Those weeks were hard, Niles, really tough. But we got through it. Together. And now you're off to work for a guy who'll probably land you in jail! Or get you killed!"

I put out my hands and reached around her waist.

"I'll be fine," I said. "It's a lot of money. Enough to—"

"No!" She dropped the basket, threw off my arms, and stepped back. "I don't care how much it is!"

"Sam, I can't pass this up."

A scowl drew her eyebrows together. She pointed a stiff finger at me.

"You leave," she said. "And I'll never forgive you."

I stepped passed her and kept my eyes straight ahead. "I'll come up and say goodbye before I go."

Chapter 7

Gary, Indiana

Thursday, April 23, 8:15 a.m.

I returned about twenty minutes later, with two Italian hoagies, a gallon of iced tea, and a couple packs of Camel unfiltered. The clerk had given me a funny look when I paid, probably because I had the look on my face of someone who had just been through a war.

Cody however, looked refreshed and very pleased with himself. He leaned against the front fender of a Nissan Pathfinder. Its burgundy paint glittered in the early-morning sunlight.

"Whadaya think of our new wheels?" he asked, and swelled proudly.

I stepped around to the front of the vehicle. A two-inch circle of cracked safety glass surrounded a small dime-size hole in the driver's side window. Blood and tiny bits of meaty tissue speckled the dashboard and steering wheel.

My knees went weak and I put my hand on the hood to steady myself. Sweat broke across my forehead and leaked down my face.

"What… " I said, in a breathy whisper. "What have you done?"

"It's got a full tank," he said. "Did I do good or what?"

I swallowed dryly and tried to comprehend.

"Who's is this?"

"Let's just say we don't hafta worry 'bout the guy reportin' it stolen. In fact, I doubt if anyone will ever find the guy."

"You… " Horror raced up my spine. "You didn't?"

"Don't feel bad, buddy, I didn't torture him or nothin'. He went easily. Slipped outta life like an oiled snake."

"You fucker!" I screamed. "You can't just kill someone! What happens in a few hours when the guy doesn't show up at home? What do you think his family's gonna do? Write him off as a loss?"

"I don't give a fuck about him or his family! I do what I hafta do to survive! I will kill any who keep me from achievin' the greatness I deserve."

"In the process you've ruined my life!"

"I saved your life!" He moved toward me with the threat of violence in his shoulders. "Two days ago you were an alcoholic, go-nowhere loser! I've given you a chance to salvage somethin' of what time you've got left on this planet! I'm givin' you a chance at achieving paradise and wealth!"

"You fucking liar!" I retorted. "You didn't bring me along to drive you to Seattle! You brought me along as an assassin's assistant! You can have the money! You can have the drugs! You can have everything! You've got your own transportation! Nothing's tied to me! I'm leaving!"

I spun around to walk away and heard the click of a weapon triggered into readiness.

"Don't take another step!" Cody warned.

A moment of silence passed so complete I discerned shrieks of waterfowl above the whistling wind and pounding surf. I turned slowly to face him and momentarily forgot how to breathe. The barrel of his .38 was aimed at my head. My lips were numb and hard to control.

"You'd kill your own friend?" I asked.

"Not so sure you're a friend anymore," Cody replied. "You still don't realize the significance of what we're achieving. You're a part of a grander thing here, buddy, about the nature of humanity and the power of individuals."

To my astonishment, the demented twinkle in his eyes dissolved and his face relaxed; like a switched had been thrown in his brain. He lowered the .38.

"Go home," he said simply.

"What?"

"Leave."

I ran my tongue along my lips. All the saliva had gone out of my mouth.

"You gonna shoot me when I turn my back?" I asked.

Cody bent over and put the gun into his ankle holster. He took a handful of napkins that came with the hoagies, opened the Pathfinder's door, and dabbed up blood from the driver's seat.

"I'm done tryin' to stop you," he said. "You want outta the fortune, so be it. But I really think you're better off stayin' with me. If you leave, I can't protect you from what will probably happen."

I straightened my shoulders. "What will happen?"

He gazed at me. "Benny will come after you. Hunt you and your family. Gun you down like vermin."

"Why would he do that?"

"You have knowledge of his existence. He knows I was comin' to see you. He knows where you live. Knows about your pretty wife. The moment you signed on for this journey she signed on, too."

"Leave her out of this!"

"She's already in it!"

"You said you're killing Benny!"

"I won't if I don't have to split the money with you. He can take his half and spare me the trouble."

Cody walked to the shoreline and tossed the blood-soaked napkins into the lake. Waves immediately swallowed them. He gazed across the huge expanse of water. Wind tugged at his shirt.

After a few moments, he turned his head. "You still here? I thought so."

I grit my teeth and spoke through them, "You know I can't go."

He smiled and then turned to face the water, again. "You wanna know how I got this way? Why I feel no remorse for my victims? There's a reason, a truly beautiful reason. Like my man Jim Morrison preached in that song,

I broke on through to the other side. Educated myself in the greatest philosophies ever written. Opened the door to the crystal clear perception I'd been searchin' for all those years in prison."

His gaze took on a miles-away fixedness.

"It started when I first got to prison. I was a nickel and dime heroin dealer locked away for twelve years in a maximum-security pen with a bunch of rapists and murderers. I don't even wanna tell you what they thought of my scrawny ass. This was before I started workin' out. Not much else to do in the Big House 'cept workout. Those first few months were rough, I mean really rough. In those days I didn't know when I left my cell in the mornin' if I'd be returnin' at night alive."

He paused, walked back over to the car, and swigged some iced tea. "Spring of my second year, two guys appeared at my cell with an undershirt soaked in vegetable oil that they'd swiped from the kitchen. They pulled their pants down, wiped the rag on their dicks, and ordered me to take my pants off and bend over. I refused. No motherfucker was gonna rape my ass while I could still throw a punch."

Cody's face twisted and he spit with disgust. "I actually did quite well fightin' 'em off. Until the noise attracted the guards. My punishment was 180 days in solitary with no exercise privilege and only one hour of television a day. 180 long days without sunlight, exercise, or human contact, just that hour of TV to distract my thoughts. 180 days of a single, constant hum from the fluorescent overheads. Can you image what that's like? Day. Night. Day. Night. Day. Night. No difference. No darkness. Just that continuous light and constant, mind-numbin' hum. It's where I came up with the frostproof."

"The what?"

"A psychological mindset where absolutely nothin' affects your emotions or lets anythin' or anyone get in the way of your own desires. You are dead to the feelin's of others." His face radiated with pleasure. "In solitary, I discovered a sense of destiny within myself, as though my life had purpose beyond the mere struggle for survival. A function that must be fulfilled. Acted upon. Perhaps..." His eyes flicked to me. "Even taught to others. Within a day of my release from this forced 180 day meditation, the guards discovered my attackers dead in their cells, their throats slashed and eyes gouged from their sockets. How's that for payback? A true orgy of unrestrained torture and my first full-blown application of the frostproof."

"That's sick!"

"Fuckers deserved everythin' I did to them. Unfortunately, the judicial system didn't agree with my form of vengeance and sent me to the prison cuckoo ward. You see, buddy, the system ain't prepared for someone of my genius. A human more advanced in the ways of natural selection. A human that will rise above the food chain into an apostle!"

"An apostle of death," I said. "I don't want to be a part of this religious bullshit!"

"The frostproof is not a religion. Religion pertains to an organization that expects a very particular set of rules and rituals be followed in order to experience God. The frostproof expands beyond that backward notion. It's man's capacity to take hold of his own development. There is no God, understand? And if there's no higher power, there's no omnipotent judge of right and wrong. That leaves the properly frostproofed person free of the burden of conscience. Free to pursue the primal side. Murder isn't the driving force, but a tool used to stay strong."

A gust scalloped the water's surface and hit me with a chilling push. Cody took out a hoagie and chewed off a bite.

"Fear no one," he said, and swallowed. "Social morality is a conspiracy of the weak rulin' class to persuade the stronger workers that it is wicked to attain power. Evil men have advanced humanity the most, have they not? Study the world's violent history; the Crusades, the fall of Rome, the Holocaust. War promotes technological development and stimulates birth, industrial growth, and economy. See how religious institutions and morality are in conflict with the actual patterns and habits of man. This contradiction surfaces as distress in the individual, causin' unhappiness and depression. We are not allowed to be the savages we have evolved from. What people consider abominable plays a vital role in the human ecosystem."

A momentary windless calm settled over us and he took the opportunity to flame up a cigarette. "Nobody suffers in this world except people who want things they can't have. With the frostproof, the individual is more important than the group. I take what I need to advance myself and comfort my sufferin', thereby makin' me greater than the populace. To be fully human, to truly experience the thrill of life, you must be a mix of animal and God." He pointed to the Pathfinder that he had taken by murder. "Anythin' less is prey."

"You don't feel anything for the people you've killed?"

"Nothing."

He tossed the remainder of his hoagie into the water.

"Enough of my preachin'. We've got more important things to do, like makin' your vehicle disappear."

* * *

Wind blew fierce along the coastal road and shook my car. I was alone in the Sentra, following Cody, who was driving the Pathfinder. We came upon a desolate inlet miles from the last small fishing town we'd passed and parked along the shoreline. Cody got out and sauntered down to the water.

I cranked the window. "Why'd you stop?"

"This looks like a good spot to drown your puppy, don'tcha think? It's nice and deep."

He motioned for me to get out and come with him. I was looking in his direction, but didn't answer. I couldn't believe we were about dump the car I'd owned for the last eight years. It bothered me in a chilling, surreal way, as if he was causing me to erase my past.

Cody came around to the trunk, withdrew our bags, and tossed them into the Pathfinder. He transferred the guns to the Pathfinder's back seat and then reached into his duffel bag and took out Jake's arm. The smell sent my stomach tumbling. Decay had eaten away part of the stump and left a bluish-black pulpy mess. Masses of white fungus threaded grotesquely between the fingers. The map was almost indecipherable.

He placed the arm on the hood of my car.

"We gotta get another bottle of rubbin' alcohol," he said, as tiny flies caught appetites and swarmed. "Gotta keep this thing from fallin' apart."

He scraped the slime off as best he could before putting the arm back into his bag.

"Leave the car running," he said. "Take the cop radio and everything from the glove compartment."

I got out as he walked around to the trunk and used the screwdriver strapped to his ankle to remove the license plate. He crumpled the plate, tossed it into the water, and then extracted the shotgun.

"Report it stolen when you get home," he said. "You got insurance, right?"

An anesthetic sense of disbelief swept through me. I scratched at my scars and felt my head nod. Cody shouldered the stock, aimed at the back windshield, and pulled the trigger. The air shuddered with explosion. A spray of glass arced into the sky and fell around the vehicle. He discharged the smoking shell, cocked, and blew out the passenger's side window. The thunderous gunshots tapered off across the lake.

He leaned in and threw the transmission into gear. The Sentra jumped forward and plowed into the lake with a huge splash. Waves creamed around the frame as it descended slowly into the muck. The engine stalled as the water overcame the hood. The front end tilted down, the back flipped up, and it slipped beneath the surf in a profusion of white bubbles.

Cody produced a cigarette, sparked it, and climbed into the Pathfinder.

I remained a statue of incredulity, unable to draw my sight from the waters circulating where the Sentra had disappeared.

"Stop reflectin' on your loss!" Cody called from the driver's side window. "Let's go!"

The inlet calmed and glimmered turquoise under the ebbing sun. I maneuvered into the passenger's side careful to avoid touching the blood of the Pathfinder's previous owner.

Chapter 8

Illinois

Thursday, April 23, 7:27 p.m.

We traveled along the perimeter of Lake Michigan, past the vegetable farms around the Kankakee River, and entered Illinois about twenty-five miles south of Chicago.

Time seemed gelled. Air felt thick and decayed.

"Stop at that telephone," I said, and pointed to an old booth lit by a streetlight.

"Who ya callin'?"

"My wife."

"Ain't you got a cell?"

"The battery died. If I don't check in she'll think something's wrong."

Cody cursed under his breath, stomped the brake, and decelerated from sixty to zero so fast I had to put out my hand to keep my head from smacking against the dashboard. I scowled at him and then opened the door.

My legs had gone to sleep and pins and needles tingled up from the bottoms of my feet.

I went into the booth, feeling an uneasy nervousness, and picked up the receiver. Cody's gaze through the windshield remained locked on me.

"Operator," a woman's voice said over the line. "How may I assist you?"

"I'd like to make a collect call to Samantha Goodman. The name's Niles."

I gave her the number and a moment of silence passed while she put the call through.

"I'm sorry, sir," the operator said. "I connected to voicemail. Please try again later."

"But— "

The line disconnected. I slammed down the receiver and turned around.

"I need change," I said. "Any in the cup holder?"

I stepped beside the Pathfinder. Cody dropped a handful of coins into my open palm. There was a little bit of blood on the coins. I put the silver in.

Voicemail picked up on the second ring: *This is the Goodman residence. Niles and Samantha aren't home right now but if you leave your name and number we'll call back as soon as we can. Thanks.*

A beep followed, and then silence.

"Sam," I said. "It's Thursday night. Things are going, uh… well. I'll be home in a few days… hope you're not still mad. I love you."

There was nothing else to say. No way I could put into words what I was going through. How close I was to losing my sanity and the moral definition between right and wrong. How the body fluids of other people were becoming as commonplace as mud.

I hung up.

"Everythin' okay?" Cody asked, as I got in and sat down in the passenger's seat.

I stared at a drop of dried blood on the dashboard. "She wasn't home."

I put shirts, pants, socks, and several pair of underwear into a gym bag and then headed into the kitchen to nab twenty dollars from the few Samantha had made in tips the previous night.

Cody sauntered in with the duffle bag hitched over his right shoulder. "Ready?"

"I hope you're right about what's out there?" I said.

"Ain't no mistake about it."

Oliver trotted up to us with tail-wagging enthusiasm. He circled Cody's legs and then hunched up and sniffed heartily at the duffel bag. Cody patted Oliver's head, and then pushed his muzzle away from the fabric. I reached into the top cabinet, grabbed the Seagrams, and stashed it into my bag.

"I only have twenty dollars," I said. "How are we going to pay for gas and food?"

"I scraped up bits of cash on the way out here," he replied. "We'll be fine." He headed toward the back kitchen door. "Let's get rollin'."

I concealed my prickling unease and went to the base of the stairs. I caught a glimpse of Samantha's unfinished sketch on the easel; an old woman gazing solemnly out a cottage window. I immediately sensed its meaning.

"Sam, I'm leaving!" I called.

She appeared at the top step. Her face, clean of makeup, was flushed and splotchy.

"You're really going?" she said. "I can't believe it!"

"Everything'll work out," I replied. "You'll see."

Her throat bobbled. "Niles, don't."

I gave a steady, firm, but loving look.

"We need a better life," I said. "This is the only way." I turned and headed toward the front. "I'll call when I can."

I opened the door and stepped out. Oliver followed.

"Oliver, stay!" I bent down and gave him a farewell ear scratch. "Watch over mama for me, okay boy?"

He licked my hand and thumped his tail. I patted his side. The night was unusually warm, full of flying insects and noisy with crickets. Moths ping-ponged around the porch light. An owl hooted.

I left Oliver and headed down the walkway toward my Sentra. Cody sat in the passenger's seat puffing on a cigarette, glaring at me through the windshield. I opened the door, tossed my bag in the back, and dropped into the driver's seat.

"How'd it go?" he asked.

"As I expected."

His hand shot out and grabbed my shoulder.

"You didn't say nothin' about where we're headin'?" He squeezed to indicate meaning. "Didja?"

I forced myself to keep from looking startled. "Of course not."

He released, rolled down the window, tossed his cigarette, snorted, and spit.

"It's all gonna be worth it, ya know?" he said. He snorted again, coughed, and lit a fresh Camel. "You got three quarters of a tank of gas. That's good. We won't have to stop for awhile."

"Is there Nicorette in the glove box?" I asked.

Cody sprung the latch. "You've got a few pieces."

I reached over and yanked off a square, then started the car, eased the transmission into reverse, and backed up the driveway. Cody seemed both relieved and elated as I shifted into drive and headed down the street. He pulled a crumpled roadmap from his back pocket, flicked on the overhead light, and smoothed the map across his thighs. Several of the creases were torn.

"Seattle's about three thousand miles from here," he said. "Averaging a conservative forty-five miles per hour and if we add in bathroom stops, food stops, and maybe a quick rest at this hotel I know, it should take us about sixty to seventy hours. We'll be in the city no later than Saturday mornin' if all goes as planned."

I nodded and thought gloriously; if all goes as planned my worries are over.

Chapter 9

Alexandria, Minnesota
Friday, April 24, 6:30 a.m.

Night passed slowly. We wound our way around Wisconsin cattle ranches and into Minnesota. I didn't quite fall asleep but my mind definitely drifted. Of all things in particular, it drifted back in time to my college days with Cody. The nights we'd stay up late, smoking marijuana and talking about the things we wanted to do with our lives. I wanted to be a famous TV chef. He wanted to be an architect so he could create monuments that would stand for ages. He'd say; "People a thousand years from now will look at my buildings and know Cody Larson had designed and built them." Then we'd drink a little, maybe smoke a little more...

I'd become so preoccupied with my thoughts, I only realized night had become morning when Cody said; "We'd better find someplace to hang until there's more traffic on the road. These bullshit nowhere towns are swarmin' with cops just achin' to pull over an out-of-state license plate. They'll pick us off like ants on a picnic lunch."

Cody's analogy stirred a memory: *the time I took Samantha to Orson's pond and we sat on an anthill by mistake. Those little buggers crawled all over us, even into our shoes. Luckily, they weren't biters. Our initial screams ended in wild laughter as we stripped off our infested clothing and jumped naked into the water.*

Cody snapped on the police radio and flipped frequencies. Intermittent transmissions crackled and popped.

"I'll figure out where the cops are and plan a route around 'em," he said.

Bags under his eyes had swollen into brown half moons.

"I wouldn't," I replied. "They're probably feeding us bogus information."

Cody grinned. "That's why I've been takin' the same route they say is bein' blocked. They wouldn't figure on us doin' that now, would they?"

The radio squawked; "231, this is command. Proceed to 94 and begin a sweep of Milford."

"Copy, Lieutenant."

"Unit 419, proceed to Alexandria."

"Copy, Lieutenant."

"I'll keep all other units informed of our progress. McGovern out."

Cody spun down the volume switch.

"They're right on top of us," he said. Tiny muscles in his face bunched. "How could that be? How could they think we'd follow their pursuit?"

Fear settled over me once again.

"I've been givin' these cops too much credit," he said. "They're dumber than I thought. They're not even tryin' to trick us! The obvious course of action is to disappear into the community until they've finished their sweep."

He sped off the next exit and turned onto a side road.

"What are you doing?" I asked. "Where are we going?"

He gripped the steering wheel and squinted. "Time to engage the frostproof."

* * *

Cody steered the Pathfinder down a rural street where low-hanging branches hid strips of overcast sky. Large country homes snuggled behind acres of preened landscaping. He slowed and scrutinized each mailbox. Then, as if one appeared somehow different from all the others, he turned down a long, paved driveway and parked halfway along the slope of a secluded property. A sweeping lawn with twirling sprinklers spread in front of a sizable, contemporary stone house. Water droplets glinted off manicured grass.

"We need new transportation," Cody said. He grabbed the bag, unzipped, and fished out two ski masks. "We need food, we need shelter, and we need to clean up. Everything we need..." He pointed to the house. "Is right in there."

"No way!" I stated defiantly. "No way am I breaking into a home!"

Cody smacked the dashboard. "I'm not fuckin' arguin' with you! We have no fuckin' time if the cops are sweepin' this area! We have to do this!"

He knotted his hands and then lowered them.

"To be fair," he said, and tossed a mask onto my lap. "I'm open to suggestions. What do you think we should do?"

I kept my gaze ahead and my mouth shut.

He cleared his throat. "Well?"

He grabbed the .38 and rested it on the dashboard in front of me. "You'll need this if you can't come up with an alternative."

I recoiled from the weapon.

"Whatcha afraid of?" he cooed. "Killin's easy. Like pullin' the wings off a fly." He looked to the house and shook his head. "I don't understand your apprehensions. Human cruelty to other humans is innate, it's part of our primal physiology; any college prof can tell you that. Here's your chance to take lives without consequence. Don'tcha wanna know what it feels like to kill? To wield the ultimate power. God's power."

He flicked his eyebrows. "Come on, buddy, taste the frostproof for the first time in your miserable, pathetic, uninspired, life. Nietzsche, Aristotle, Napoleon, Hitler; I've read about them all; all the great men who have imprinted their essence upon the consciousness of society. I learned somethin' from each of them. A little secret that caused those human beings to shine far above all others of their era. You wanna know what that is?"

My sight remained glued to the weapon on the dashboard.

He continued. "Those men realized what they are, wild animals in a society wrought with ethical cages. In nature, the strongest, the creature willin' to take the greatest risks, that creature gains the most rewards, the most power; becomes the leader of the pack. Society restrains the human condition in ways you cannot comprehend because you, buddy, are a part of the problem, not a part of the solution. In seeking to become like everyone else, you've lost that predatory, will-to-conquer impulsiveness predisposed to animals of this planet. All animals!"

He dug out a hair band from his front pocket and tied back his mop. "You consider my motives evil because they're outside the norm of your conditionin'. When you unlearn everythin' you've been taught by our educational and religious systems you'll begin to comprehend the true nature of man."

His words made me want to run from the car, burst into the house, and warn the people inside. *"Get out!"* I'd scream. *"There's a madman coming and he's going to slaughter you! And I can't help you! I can't!"*

I was scared shitless for the family but I was also scared for myself. I was beginning to understand and rationalize Cody's philosophical ramblings. I was beginning to see things from his warped perspective. I could accept violence against innocents as part of our self-preservation.

"Humans have reached a state of crisis tryin' to live in a civilization," he continued. "Government laws forbid primal outlets, causin' people to restrain the violence that comes natural to them. They push their depraved feelin's down, deep down, where the emotions eat away at their insides. They drift through life wonderin' why they feel so empty. Wonderin' what the meanin' of their existence is, because they can't find outlets to satisfy their buried, incarnate desires. I live in a world without government control or religion's squeaky-clean morality. The free exercise of my primality is what separates me from the masses. Makes me stronger!"

He donned the ski mask and clicked off the .45's safety.

"We have the advantage of total surprise here," he said. "Don't blow it by doin' somethin' spontaneous and stupid."

He started to give the .38 back to me but I pushed his hand away.

"I won't be a part of this!" I said. "You're on your own."

"Get out of the vehicle," he snarled. "I'm not tellin' ya again."

I stared at the house resting in early-morning silence at the bottom of the hill.

Cody held out the gun. "Take it!"

"I won't!"

He grabbed my hand, wrapped my fingers around the grip, and shoved the ski mask into my chest.

"I'm gettin' tired of your resistance!" he stated. "Now follow me or become one of them... one of the weak."

He appraised me with a burning stare and then got out of the Pathfinder.

I put on the ski mask and nearly retched from the putrid odor absorbed into the fabric off the rotting arm. I may have been the only person in the world that could possibly save the people inside this house, but if they got a look at my face, I'd have no one to save me.

* * *

Cody crept through the woods with a practiced silence toward the house. I on the other hand made a lot of noise crunching on sticks and snapping small branches.

"Watch me," he instructed. He leapt from a rock, to a patch of dirt, to a stump, hardly making a sound. "Look for clear spots and mud."

We approached and crouched under a half-open window. The sound of water pellets drumming against linoleum drifted out. Someone was taking a shower.

"At least we know where one of 'em is," Cody whispered. He raised his head slowly to peer through the screen. "Looks like a four bedroom place so there's bound to be a kid around, maybe two. Don't worry 'bout them until after the parents are secured."

"I'm not doing this!" I whispered harshly.

He grabbed my shirtsleeve and twisted it. "You are!"

A man passed the window. Cody pulled me down. After a moment, Cody raised his head and pulled me up by my sleeve to look into the room with him. Clothes and undergarments littered the floor. A large wood dresser against the far wall was covered with family pictures. Two nightstands loaded with books and boating magazines were on either side of a king-size bed. One had a telephone on top. A ceiling fan rotated slowly.

"This must be the master bedroom," Cody said. "This saves us from solvin' one problem. Somethin' you can always count on when it comes to infiltratin' families in the morning, there's usually a parent in the kitchen while the other's in the shower. Always seems to happen that way. Oh, and make sure you take out the phone before you head into the bathroom. We don't want anyone on the outside world knowing we're here."

My pulse banged in my ears.

"I won't do this," I whispered.

"You must!" he hissed. "Let go of your societal conditionin' and allow yourself to become the savage within. You'll switch on your primal programmin' when under a crisis situation, trust me."

"No!"

He thrust his face close to mine. Muscles in his jaw pulsed. "Use a blunt object to bash in their heads if you have to. We've gotta work together on this or we're both fucked, understand? Both of us!"

My skin went cold.

"The signal'll be the sound of breakin' glass," he added fiercely.

"Signal?"

He sighed deeply through his nostrils. "Do I have to explain every fuckin' thing to you? The signal that the house is secure. The sound of breakin' glass'll bring out whoever's in the shower. That's when you come into play. Make certain you get through the screen window before anyone gets out of the bathroom or this is gonna get real messy. Remember, listen for the sound of breaking glass first."

He crept around the corner of the house.

A few seconds later, I heard the doorbell chime. My heart jack-hammered as I crouched lower in the shrubbery.

A long moment of silence passed.

Gripped by an almost irresistible urge to take off running, I held back the impulse. Knowing if I did I'd be running for the rest of my life.

Footsteps and noises banged through the house followed by quick, panicky shouts for help just outside the bedroom. Then more silence.

I jumped up and pressed my face against the screen.

No sound of breaking glass.

The shower water shut off.

"Norm?" a woman's voice called from the bathroom. "Norm? Honey? You okay?"

My body slicked over with sweat.

"Honey?"

Not so much as a sound from behind the closed bedroom door. I stood weak-kneed debating what to do.

Then I heard it.

A faint crash; like a dropped light bulb; the unmistakable chime of shattered glass.

My heart pounded in my temples. Only one outcome was certain now. If I stayed outside the window everyone in this house would die.

* * *

I quickly punched in the screen, heaved up, and pulled my body inside.

Shades rustled.

Sweat leaked down the back of my neck.

"Who's there?" the woman in the bathroom called. "Norm? Norm, are you okay?"

The room smelled of soap, shampoo, and Old Spice aftershave, providing slight relief from the rancid rot-odor effused in the ski mask. I hurried to the dresser and pulled the telephone cord from the wall. It sprung back and almost hit me in the head.

"Norm? Hello? Norm?"

I inhaled a few quick breaths, steadied my nerves, and then crept into the bathroom. A long, pink robe hanging on the inside of the door stirred as I passed. I crossed a marble counter laden with cosmetics and moved toward the stall shower. Through the translucent curtain, I saw a small, shapely woman wiping excess water from her body. She flung her plume of hair back and whooshed the plastic aside. We locked sight in a split-second, terrifying gaze. Her eyes snapped into O's of terror. She shrieked, reached out and grabbed a curling iron, and raised it to use as a weapon.

My primal programming switched on.

I lunged and wrapped my arms around her slippery body. The curling iron crashed to the tile floor. She squirmed and tore wildly at my hair and my ski mask. Her shrieks burned in my ears. Our feet tangled and we slipped to the floor. My breath knocked away as I absorbed the shock of her weight.

"Stop!" I wheezed, and held on.

I knew if I let go and she ran screaming out of the room, Cody would kill her. I threw my legs over hers to hold her in place and clasped her shoulders. Muscles in her body tightened. She stared at me with horror-struck eyes. Tears broke and began streaming down her cheeks.

I clamped my hand over her mouth. "Shh!"

"Oh God!" she gasped through my fingers.

"I'm trying to protect you!" I said the words so forcefully she actually stopped struggling and lay trembling.

"From what?" she sobbed.

Cody barreled into the room.

"Where's the kids?" he shouted. "Where's the kids? Where's the fuckin' kids?"

He pulled me off her, slammed his boot-heel against her sternum, and knelt forward, putting most of his weight on her chest.

"You stinkin', slutty, lyin' bitch! Where's the fuckin' kids!"

"Cody, stop!" I shouted.

He raised his gun and aimed at my heart. "Don't say my name!"

He turned back to the woman and twisted his foot. The woman's skin tore between her breasts. Her eyes squeezed shut. She gasped. Her face was wild and red.

"There are two bedrooms filled with kids' shit! Where are they?"

The woman struggled to breathe and Cody eased up on his heel.

"You got somethin' to tell me?" he asked.

"They're..." She wheezed and sobbed. "They're... they're at a friend's. My husband and I are alone."

"Liar!" Cody's hand slashed across her face.

I lunged at him and he smacked the side of my head with the pistol; whacked me so hard I saw stars.

"What do ya think you're doin'?" he hollered at me. "I'm workin' here!"

"Get off her!"

"Stay out of this!" He snatched his screwdriver and focused on the woman. "I haven't tortured anyone in a while, but it's like ridin' a bike, you never really forget."

He punctured the flesh above her right breast. She drew back and flailed her hands protectively across her chest. He smacked them away.

"Where are the kids?"

"I'm telling the truth!" she cried. "They won't be dropped off 'til tomorrow! I swear to God! Swear to Jesus! Please!"

"Lay off her!" I stepped forward, rubbing the rising lump on my temple. "You're not doing this!"

Cody flashed me a look so cold it could have frozen saltwater. He clasped the woman's throat in a stranglehold.

"If she's lyin' to us and her little snot kids are runnin' to the neighbors to call the cops, we're all gonna be dead."

She shook her head urgently against his grip.

"Truth!" she gasped. Gagging sounds emanated from her throat. "Swear!"

"If it ain't," he said. "You're life is over."

He released and the woman's hands flew to her neck. She breathed with huge gusts.

He turned to me. "Next time you interrupt me when I'm beginnin' the frostproof somethin' bad's gonna happen to someone! Got that?"

I wanted to punch Cody in the face. I wanted to put a bullet into his brain. I wanted to put a knife through his heart.

I nodded slowly.

His eyes wandered the woman's naked body.

"Sure you don't wanna have a little party while we got her like this?" he encouraged, with a wink. "Live out a few sick fantasies? Here's your chance to rape like a wild animal and no one would ever know, 'cept for me, of course."

I glared at him. He got off her and I helped her to a sitting position, then took a towel and wrapped it around her trembling shoulders.

"We're not doing any more harm to this woman!" I stated, and guided her up and into the bedroom.

Cody followed out and headed down the hallway.

The moment he disappeared, the woman squirmed from my hands, jumped at a lamp, grabbed it, and swung it above her head.

"Get away from me!" she screamed.

Until three days ago, I'd never in a million years have threatened someone with a gun. But now… Cody was beginning to influence my behavior, my actions. I was getting to be more like him and I feared that the most. I withdrew the pistol and shook it at the woman. She burst into sobs and let the lamp slip from her fingers. I stuffed the pistol back into my waistband feeling absolutely sick about the whole situation.

"I'm sorry," I said, and shook my head. "You don't understand. If you don't cooperate he's going to kill you, plain and simple. Now, please, put on some clothes and do what he says. I promise I'll keep you from harm."

I glanced at a framed photo of a slim, smiling man with a receding hairline standing beside a watery expanse glimmering pinkish with early evening sun. The man's eyes appeared to twinkle behind thick eyeglasses. He seemed very happy.

Cody returned before the woman could put on anything more than pants and a bra. He took her arm and pulled her into the kitchen where the same man from the photograph sat slumped unconscious against the wall beside a pair of broken eyeglasses. Electrical cord bound his arms and legs. Blood trickled from the side his head and flowed along his jaw.

The woman went hysterical when she saw him.

"Shut up!" Cody shouted. "Shut the fuck up! I have a fuckin' headache!"

Her shriek tapered and she collapsed into hushed tears beside the man.

"You gotta beautiful place here," Cody said. He sauntered toward a large bay window that overlooked the driveway. "Real nice." He spun around and aimed his .38 at the woman's head. "What's your name?"

She answered with a guttural wail.

"Listen, bitch, I'm tryin' to be civil here! And you have no idea how hard I'm tryin'. Now, what the fuck is your name?"

The woman sniffed and opened and closed her mouth as she tried to form words. "Glo... Glo... Gloria. Gloria Peterson."

Cody pointed with the barrel. "And this guy?"

"N... Norman."

"Well, Gloria Peterson, we seem to have developed a bit of a situation here. See, we were just gonna borrow your house for a little while and maybe take your car until my inexperienced partner over there said my name out loud which translates into you bein' able to tell the cops who did this." His mouth twitched as he approached her. "I gotta make certain you don't."

Gloria's face turned a mask of terror. "I won't tell! I won't tell!"

"You will eventually," Cody said. "Y'all do."

He winked at me and raised the .38.

"Stop!" I made a move toward him and he whipped the gun in my direction.

"Don't!" he warned. "This is a valuable lesson I'm teaching ya."

"Put the gun down," I said.

"Sorry, can't do that. People will say anything to live. I don't trust what my victims promise. It's one of the rules of the frostproof."

He aimed the muzzle at her head.

Already pale, Gloria's face turned the color of chalk.

"Do you believe in God?" he asked. "A great creator who may or may not be watchin' over us at this very moment? A judge of all things good and evil and moral. Father and keeper of our souls for eternity? Do ya? Do ya believe?"

Gloria's eyes fastened firmly on the floor.

"Yes," she said, in barely a whisper. "I believe."

He stepped toward her. "And do ya think a man like me, an assassin, the incarnation of evil, is a mistake of God's? If there is such a being?"

She cringed and shook her head slowly from side to side. "Why are you asking me these questions?"

"If God is incapable of makin' mistakes," Cody preached. "Then how do you explain me? You wanna know what I think? I think God is a mistake of man's. I don't think He exists at all. And you know what? You're gonna find out in about ten seconds."

Cody turned and talked in my direction. "See where your carelessness has gotten these people, buddy?" He yanked off his ski mask and threw it to the floor. "I've been tellin' ya all along how important it is to watch whatcha do and say. How the littlest mistakes can fuck us. But do ya listen? No! You keep tellin' me not to kill." He took on a poor, high-pitched mocking of my voice. "Don't kill people, Cody! Don't kill! It's wrong! It's wrong!"

He tousled Gloria's hair, then grabbed a tuft and yanked back her head. He pressed the barrel against her temple.

"No!" I shouted.

My feet pushed off the ground and I threw my body into him knocking us both off-balance. The gun fired with a thunderous bang and the hallway mirror shattered.

Cody punched me in the face and I rolled off him. He hopped up and kicked my side. Hard.

"Have you lost your fuckin' mind!" he hollered, and re-leveled the gun at Gloria's head. "Do that again, buddy and you're dead!"

"Don't!" I stated, breathing heavy, my cheek aching, my body full of tremble. "Please don't do this!"

His mouth twitched. A far-away fixedness took over his gaze. "Sorry, buddy, I know this is tough to take, but despite whatcha may think of me, I didn't kill these people, you did. You did because ya didn't think before ya spoke. Keep it up and we'll both end up in a casket."

He looked at me and pulled the trigger.

The hammer clicked.

Gloria's features drew tight and then relaxed.

"Shit," Cody said. "Out of bullets."

He laughed, and the sound filled the air like cyanide gas. He pulled a clip from his back pocket and slapped it into the magwell.

"Only had one in the chamber," he said. "I was curious what you would do. Now I know. You're still not properly frostproofed."

I swallowed dryly.

"Hope ya learned somethin' today, buddy," he added. "Watch your mouth."

I nodded absently, numb with relief. Gloria's saucer-sized eyes blinked several times, and then she fainted.

* * *

I sat in the Peterson's living room, feeling half-delusional. I couldn't believe where I was or what I was doing. It was like the worst nightmare I'd ever experienced playing out in real life.

Cody secured Gloria with rope and extension cords and then went outside to move the Pathfinder around to the back of the house. I walked into the living room. Norman Peterson's breathing had become rapid. His flesh looked bluish, as if he'd been soaking in a tub of cold water. His lips were pale.

"You," Gloria said.

Every muscle in my body stiffened at the sound of her voice.

"Help us!" she begged. "Please!"

Her eyes were panicky and pleading and tears streamed from them.

"I… I can't," I said.

"At least help Norm. He's diabetic. He needs his shot. I know you've got compassion. Please let me give him his shot."

I scratched at my scars and shook my head. "If I do he'll kill us all."

Gloria struggled against the restraints only to slump forward dejectedly.

Cody stormed in and hurled his duffle bag onto the coffee table sending a lamp flying to the floor. The bulb exploded.

Dank odor oozed through the bag's fabric and quickly filled the room. Cody unzipped and withdrew Jake's arm, which was encased in a fuzzy glove of white mold.

Gloria turned her head and retched.

Cody took the arm and went into the kitchen. A few moments later, he came back holding a ceramic bowl.

"Hungry?" he asked me. "Looks like some kinda' pasta salad. I saw it when I put the arm in the fridge."

I stepped toward him.

"Norman is in pretty bad shape," I said. "He needs insulin."

Cody reached into the bowl with the same grimy hand that had held the arm. Pieces of mold still stuck on his fingers.

"You two been talkin' while I was outside?" he asked. "What other lies has she told you?"

I blinked owlishly. "Lies?"

"If you believe the shit she's saying, you're even stupider than I thought."

"What harm can— "

"No! They stay like this until I say! These two are lucky to still be alive. Keepin' hostages goes against everythin' the frostproof has taught me about survivin'!"

He shoveled a handful of noodles into his mouth and chewed slowly.

"Have some compassion, for God's sake!" I stated.

"Compassion!" he spat. "Fuck that! No one ever showed me any when I was in trouble!"

* * *

Two hours slipped by that felt like two days. Norman Peterson's breath went in and out of him in raspy gasps. Dark semi-circles had formed in the flesh under his closed eyes. Blood had coagulated on his cheeks and chin.

I sat on the couch and stared at the second hand while it crept around the glassy face of the wall clock. Cody paced in front of the bay window twisting his hands and flinching whenever the house creaked or a noise emitted from outside. He looked through the slit in the mini blinds for the hundredth time and then took another fast look.

"Untie her!" he stated. "Quick! Cut the cords!"

"What's happening?" I asked.

"The police are here!"

It was as if someone had plugged me into an electrical socket. My whole body came alive with a surge of energy and adrenaline. I scrambled toward the couple, my legs feeling like rubber. Cody grabbed a kitchen knife and slid it across the floor toward me. He snatched a towel and dabbed Norman's blood from the floor.

"Cut her free!" he stated. "Hurry! Hurry!"

He clamped his hand around Gloria's neck as I sawed through the bindings.

"Show any sign that we're here," he said menacingly, into her ear. "And the first thing I'm gonna do after I drop the cop is put a bullet into your sweet hubby's head. Got it?"

She nodded rapidly under his grip. He removed his hand leaving momentary finger marks.

"Hold this," he said, and pushed his .38 into my palm. "I'll be right back."

He grabbed Norman under the arms and dragged his limp body into the downstairs bathroom. Gloria's eyes locked with mine.

"Now's your chance!" she urged. "I'll tell the cops you're innocent! I will! I promise! I'll tell them you saved us! That you're a hero! Please! Please, help us!"

"Sit tight," I said. "It's almost over."

"You have a gun! Use it! Use it against him!"

I leaned back to look into the room where Cody had taken Norman.

"Please! Please help us!"

I thought about it. Seriously thought about blowing Cody away when he came back into the room. Aiming the gun as he walked in, before he could react. *Could I do it? Could I really do it?* My finger found the safety and flicked it off.

Cody rushed from the bathroom carrying a blue bath towel and snatched the .38 from my grip. He threw Gloria the towel.

"Listen carefully," he said to her. "You're gonna answer the door, be polite, and say everythin's fine and dandy here. You're havin' a good ol' American mornin'. Then wish the cops the same, say goodbye, and close the door. If you fuck up even a tiny bit, everyone's gonna die."

He waggled the barrel in my direction. "'Cept him, of course. You go upstairs. Whatever happens, don't come down til I say. I mean it!"

Concern rose into my mind. I gave him a long look and then trotted to the top of the steps and crouched where I could observe what was happening.

Cody pushed Gloria to the front door and placed the muzzle between her shoulder blades.

A few seconds later, a knock echoed through the house and then the ding of the doorbell. Cody motioned for her to open it. As she did, milky morning sunlight and the sound of chattering birds filled the entranceway; so did a tall police officer with a young face and pleasant expression.

"Greetings, ma'am," the officer said. "How are you this morning?"

Gloria stood mutely, as if she'd forgotten how to speak. She looked pale, frightened, and haggard.

"Is there a problem, officer?" she managed to ask.

"State police business, ma'am," the officer replied. "We've been asked to speak with residents in the neighborhood and warn folks of a felon who's been tracked to this area. We're advising folks to keep their windows and doors locked and to report any suspicious activity, no matter how insignificant or trivial it may seem."

Gloria nodded slowly, mechanically. Her whole body shook. The officer's expression crimped into one of concern.

"Ma'am, is everything all right?"

Cody drilled the .38 into her side.

"What? Yes... yes. Everything's fine. You've caught me at an awkward moment, that's all. My kids are away and my... my husband and I are having sort of an adult morning."

A smile overspread the police officer's face. He tipped his hat. "Yes ma'am, I understand. I won't take up any more of your time. Have a good day now."

The officer strolled back to his cruiser.

Cody bumped the door shut with his elbow, holstered the gun, and started clapping, slowly at first, but then harder and louder as brake lights faded from the window.

"Extraordinary performance," he said. "You deserve an award."

He grabbed the base of Gloria's neck, pulled her head back, and forced his lips to hers. She attempted to whip her arms around to break free. He pulled her head back more and tore off the towel. She let out a shrill, panicked scream and began to sob.

"No!" I raced down the steps barely aware of my feet.

He forcibly wrestled her to the floor.

"Get off her!" I hollered and stopped just short of barreling him over.

Cody ripped down her bra and the cut above her breast spilled blood.

"Off!" I screamed.

He jumped to his feet seething with anger.

"The only reason I haven't killed this bitch is because I still have respect for your morality and fragility! Don't blow it by restrainin' my primal urges! Let me have my fun!"

"It's wrong!"

"Right and wrong don't exist in my world!"

"They do in mine!"

I stared at him; eye to eye; stared him down.

Cody turned away, plopped on the couch, and released a loud lungful of breath. Gloria was sobbing.

"Let me explain somethin' to ya, buddy," he said. "The frostproof has rules. And rule number one is don't ever get emotionally attached to your enemy. Ya think this bitch really cares if you live or die? She'd be just as happy to see you on the ground with blood streamin' from your head. Rule two is don't believe anythin' your enemy says. And rule three, perhaps the most important, is always keep rules one and two a top priority. Am I makin' myself clear?"

"Sometimes you have to break rules to make certain you win the game," I said, and helped Gloria to her feet. "Where's the insulin?"

* * *

Norman Peterson regained consciousness around 4:00 p.m., much to my and Gloria's relief. He looked dazed, and his head dawdled to one side, but he seemed vaguely aware of the couple's dreadful predicament.

"Okay, buddy," Cody said, and sauntered into the room. "Pull yourself together cause we're headin' out." He inhaled a deep breath and fixed his gaze in the Petersons' direction. "Whadaya think we should do 'bout these two?"

Gloria's eyelids widened. Norman stared at the wall in an almost catatonic state.

"Leave them!" I stated, and hurried across the room toward the door. "Let's go!"

Cody cocked his head and massaged his fingers over the stubble on his chin. "Ya think that's a wise idea? Just leavin' 'em here like this? These people are our enemies. Until you and I part ways, everyone we come in contact with is our enemy."

Cody sauntered into the kitchen and returned with the arm.

"If ya really think I shouldn't frostproof 'em," he said, and buried Jake's arm into the bag. "Then I'll go along with your choice… this time. We're gonna have to start trustin' each other's judgments if we're gonna make it through this shit. But, ya do realize she's gonna call the cops the second she escapes our bindings."

"We'll tie the knots tight."

"If we don't frostproof 'em we can' t trust taking their car without them reportin' it to the cops. And they've got a nice new Jeep Cherokee that could probably get us to where we need to go without a problem. We've been in the same vehicle for over a day, that's pushin' it. Odds are we'll be stopped at some point along the way. You prepared for what might happen?"

"Let's go!"

"Wastin' 'em would give us many worry-free hours."

I set my jaw, squared my shoulders, and shook my head. "No!"

"Guess you're willin' to test the limits," he said, and smacked his lips. "Okay, buddy, it's your call, your decision. But if anything unexpected happens, I'm going to unleash the frostproof on whoever gets in our way."

* * *

Cody tied the Petersons tight and then loaded the Pathfinder. I went on a whirlwind search of the house to make certain the telephone lines were cut, the shades were drawn, and all the doors and windows were locked against snooping neighbors or another visit by the police. We needed to put as much time between us and the Peterson's before they freed themselves.

I went into the kitchen to maybe get something into my stomach and ease the dull, constant hunger pang. I opened the refrigerator, got a rancid blast of arm-rot smell, and closed the door in disgust.

I discovered a bottle of Absolut vodka in the cabinet above the kitchen sink. The thought of drinking it or any alcoholic beverage now disgusted me and I returned to the base of the stairs a sober, emotional wreck. Cody had come back inside with the shotgun. A menu of expressions rolled over his face as he stared at the Petersons. His upper lip twitched.

"I'm only gonna warn you folks this one time," he said. "If I find out you've called the cops at any point from now into the future… "

He aimed at the downstairs bathroom door and fired from the hip. Wood splintered and the door exploded off its hinges, shaking the house with concussion. Sawdust and the smell of gunpowder discharge polluted the air.

"I'm gonna come back and finish what I started! That's a permanent promise with no expiration date, got it?"

Gloria signaled a pitiful yes with her eyes. I tried not to think about the situation, just mentally float away to an ethereal dream where I could ignore Cody's behavior.

He headed outside and I heard the Pathfinder's engine rumbled to life.

"Hurry your ass up!" he shouted.

I crossed the living room and paused by the front door.

"I wish I could have done more to help," I said, and went out.

Once in the Pathfinder, I peeled off the ski mask and scratched my face for a good ten seconds. Cody started up the driveway and then stomped on the brakes. My head nearly slammed against the dashboard.

"What's wrong with you?" I exclaimed.

His face was a stone carving of dubiety.

"Were ya thinking of takin' me out back there?" he questioned, his gaze dissecting me. "Were ya thinkin' of killin' me?"

Fear sunk into my bones. My face got hot.

"Of course not," my voice quavered. "Why?"

"Don't try to deceive me 'cause you'll lose! My intellect is as sharp as a fuckin' stiletto! I heard what your precious charity case said when I left the room." He pointed the .38 at my chest. "Every fuckin' word that bitch said about how she'd tell the cops you're innocent and it was all my doin'."

My insides turned to jelly.

"I wasn't going to turn against you," I said. "I swear!"

His eyes didn't change their focus. "So why's the safety off?"

Silence lingered into seconds. My pores grew lush with sweat that dribbled down my cheeks.

"That's what I thought." He put the Pathfinder into gear and we proceeded up the driveway. "Honesty… that's all that I ask. I understand your impulse and forgive you. That may have been your best chance to take me out and get away with it and ya didn't. It's a good thing, too, because if you'd decided to go against me… " He patted his left ankle. "I still got this."

A sense of lucid relief swept over me. I exhaled, causing a momentary ghostly film of condensation to erupt across the windshield and distort my view.

We pulled onto the road and continued west of St. Paul, Minnesota, under a chilly, ash-gray sky.

Chapter 10

Rolla, North Dakota
Saturday, April 25, time unknown

The dirt road we turned onto was remote and in dismal condition and we struggled to maintain 20 mph. The police radio hissed white noise, occasionally interrupted by a squelch of static, and sometimes a voice; but we paid little attention. I even suggested that we chuck the device into the woods. But Cody insisted we keep it. He said we'd have use for it later, but wouldn't say for what.

As the late day sun slid toward the edge of the world, Cody became even more determined to reach Seattle. The latest forecast for the Pacific Northwest called for a steady, drenching rain and the weather had put a scare into him. Now he feared the entire loot could get washed away.

Dreadfully exhausted, I actually fell asleep, undisturbed by the sounds and bumps.

I'm my college self.

I'm in sociology class. Students are facing me, but their blank, wide-eyed stares are focused on something else. I follow their collective gaze to the front of the room where Samantha lies in the center of an expanding pool of blood. Only the blood isn't red, it's black. She's moaning, but the sound isn't coming from her mouth, it's coming from a gaping hole in her belly. Her inner organs are making the noise.

Someone shouts; a familiar, gruff voice.

I twirl my head to see Cody standing behind me with his mouth curved into a comically-wide grin. His eyes are gleaming red and his cobra tattoo is alive and writhing, coiled around his neck.

I turn back to the front. Samantha is still wounded, but now standing to the side. The body in the front of the room has changed into my likeness. The throat is cut and a line of blood is draining from its mouth. Its eyes are glazed and still.

"Hey, buddy," Cody coos. "Wanna take some pot shots at yourself?"

He opens his hand to reveal a .38, its muzzle speckled with oversized droplets of black blood. Suddenly, there's black blood spread all over his shirt. There's black blood on Samantha. There's black blood on my hands and arms and in my mouth. I spit black blood.

"Jacob," the other me gurgles from its slit throat. "You must save Jacob!"

Flames spring up around me as fire engulfs the room. Somehow the .38 is now in my hand.

"Yessssss," Cody hisses. "Feel the frostproof! Feel the frostproof flow through your veins!"

My hand rises as if being controlled by someone else.

I can't stop!
I aim at Samantha's head.
Her face is sallow, full of fear and horror.
Her eyes are jittering.
Cody's mouth is twitching.
"Feel the frostproof, feel the frostproof," he purrs.
My finger applies pressure to the trigger.
I can't stop!
Samantha screams.
Cody laughs. "Feel the frostproof!"
I can't stop my finger!
Bam!

I jarred awake.

* * *

Dawn lightened the sky with a pink haze as the sun rose over the distant mountain. I had slept through the night.

We continued along endless roads through North Dakota wheat fields finally stopping for food and gas at a roadside market/bait shop. We ate sandwiches, filled the tank, and then continued into Montana.

For hours, I listened to the drone of the tires against the asphalt, the gusty flow of wind over the car. It felt as if I were observing what was happening from the outside, as if this person traveling along with Cody wasn't me, but a figment of my imagination; an actor playing the role of a fictional character in a fictional story.

The Rocky Mountains came upon us like a massive ridge of gray glaciers capped with white snow. The roadway turned quickly from a slight rise into a sharp diagonal gradient. The Pathfinder's engine wheezed and sputtered under the continuous strain of going up. Finally, it blatted two loud backfires and stalled.

I buried my face in my hands and scratched my forehead with my fingertips. Cody jumped out of the Pathfinder and unlatched the hood. A puff of white smoke curled into the sky.

"Fuck!" he screamed. "Head gasket's blown! I can see the oil! I knew we shoulda' killed those fuckin' Petersons and taken their Jeep! I knew it! Fuck! Fuck! Fuck!"

His fist hit the fender repeatedly and he stomped his feet like a child in the depths of a tantrum. "I should have killed those people and taken their Jeep! I knew I should have wasted them! I knew it! I knew it! The frostproof is always right! Always!"

"Can we rig it?" I asked, trying to dilute his rage with reason.

He peered at me with eyes blazing the intensity of rocket boosters.

"I don't think you fully understand what's happened here, buddy," he replied. "It's frostproof time for the next person we meet."

* * *

Shadows stretched across the road. Time flowed like sludge. I sat on the hood in a trance-like state, almost as catatonic as Norman Peterson had been. I was scared.

Scared for the fate of someone I'd never met. Scared for whoever happened to come upon us.

Cody paced back and forth across the road, spouting obscenities. Every so often, I heard the words, "kill" "should've"_and "frostproof" among his babble.

The sudden grumble of an approaching police cruiser rounding the bend about a quarter-mile away caught my attention. I stared at the oncoming vehicle as it headed up the incline, so terrified I had to drive my fingernails into my palms to hold myself together and keep from rushing into the woods. Cody saw it, too. He filled his hands with mud and smeared it over the license plate and back bumper then crawled underneath the Pathfinder's chassis.

I slid off the hood, my heart banging. The cruiser drew closer, and then slowed.

I breathed a gigantic sigh of relief. It wasn't a police cruiser as I'd thought, though the body style of the vehicle was almost identical in appearance, but a park ranger. The ranger's vehicle eased up to us and the window rolled down.

"Afternoon," the ranger said. Gray hair capped a disarming face set with clean blue eyes that got squinty as he smiled. "You boys alright?"

"It's the engine," I said. "My friend's checking it out."

"Then why's he looking in the back?"

Cody wiggled out and stood. He wiped his muddy hands on his pants and shot me a quick look indicating my stupidity.

"Checkin' the brakes, too," he replied. "They felt loose."

The ranger shut off his ignition and stepped from the car. His expression remained pleasant and unassuming.

"Where ya boys from?" he asked.

"Vermont," Cody replied.

"That's a long ways from here. Where're ya heading?"

"Oregon."

"That's a long ways, too. Open the hood, let's have a look."

Cody nodded for me to do it. He stepped around to the front with the .38 palmed in his right hand.

Blood stained the fabric covering the passenger's side door and I moved to block the view of it and the stolen police radio as I reached through the window and flipped the latch. The ranger lifted the hood and leaned into the engine.

"You've got problems, all right," he said. "Oil's squirting through the head gasket. This thing's gonna need some shop time."

"Too bad there ain't one close by," Cody said, and positioned to get a better shot.

My throat dried up. I shook my head for him not to do it.

"But there is," the ranger said. He closed the hood and strode to his car. "Hop in, I'll take ya to town. It's just a few miles south. We'll get my brother to tow this to his shop. Guaranteed he'll have ya up and running in no time."

Cody and I both looked at each other. He shrugged, leaned down out of the ranger's sight, and slid the pistol back into his ankle holster.

"I'm assumin' this is what you want?" Cody muttered to me. "Rather than to use the frostproof?"

I glared at him. "No one gets hurt."

"I can't promise that. But I do agree we can't be drivin' around in a municipal vehicle."

Cody went to the Pathfinder's trunk.

"Is it okay if we bring our stuff?" he asked.

"Wouldn't worry about nobody stealing in these parts," the ranger replied.

"Call it excessive paranoia," Cody said. He snatched his bag and my gym bag. "I like to keep my possessions close."

"Suit yourself."

Cody put our items into the ranger's trunk and we folded into the backseat. The car reeked from a merger of our sweat and the spoiled arm. I shuffled uncomfortably on the worn vinyl.

"We really appreciate this," I said, as the car pulled out. "We didn't expect to be in this situation."

"No one does," the ranger replied. "You'd be surprised how many motorists underestimate the toll these mountains take on their vehicles."

We turned onto a paved road that ran along a high ridge. Shades of squared-off property sewed a colorful landscape in the green valley below.

"Sumneytown," the ranger informed us. "Population three-thousand two-hundred and twenty-seven. Twenty-eight if you count what's growing in Betsy Whittaker's belly. Lived here all my life. See that large white building? My two girls were born— "

"Attention all units in the vicinity of Rockford County," the ranger's radio squawked. "Be advised of a dangerous— "

The ranger flicked off the device. His eyes flashed up to the rearview mirror. Cody put his hand to the holster on his ankle.

"Always something stirring up there in Rockford County," the ranger said. "Ever since they built the prison in '72. Anyways, as I was saying, my two girls... "

I stopped listening and concentrated on keeping my wits about me. I was determined not to let harm come to this man or any others, even if that meant battling Cody. Enough was enough.

The ranger turned onto what must have been the town's main street since it was the only one with a sidewalk and sporadic streetlights. Faces turned toward us as we cruised down the strip. People smiled and waved.

"Sumneytown's a great place to raise a family," the ranger said. "I'm sure you gentlemen will enjoy your unforeseen stay. We have a movie theater and there's a small amusement park just down the south side that's got a Ferris wheel."

"We don't plan on stayin' long," Cody said. "We've got commitments."

"By the looks of your engine I betcha I'll be seeing ya out at Rosa's Diner come six o'clock. She pulls the prime rib from the oven 'round then. Meat cuts with a fork. The food'll be worth the lost night, trust me."

We steered into a rundown gas station that looked as if it were designed after a Norman Rockwell painting. Long strips of gray siding were peeling from the building's walls. A warped aluminum overhang kept two rusted 1950's-style gas pumps dry. Oil stains tattooed the cement.

"This is it," the ranger said.

He beeped the horn.

A tall, slim man with a deep-water tan, wearing blue coveralls spotted with grease appeared at the doorway of the rickety building. A cigarette poked from the corner of his mouth.

"Go ahead and show Reese where your vehicle is," the ranger said. "I'll stop back later to see how everything's going. If ya need a place to stay, the Sumneytown Lodge always has a vacancy. Nice rooms, too. Got cable TV and a heated pool."

We stepped out and took our bags. Cody appeared tense. He withdrew the neon green sports watch and checked the time. His jaw tightened.

"Good luck with everything," the ranger said.

He beeped farewell and drove off.

Cody started a slow, sludgy walk toward the building. I followed beside him.

"We can't let him do this," he muttered. "As soon as this guy checks the plates and vin number, we're fucked."

"He won't check," I whispered. "He'll just fix it."

"We can't take that chance. You didn't want me to take out that sweet old man now, didja? Someone here has to go. It's just the way it is."

I stopped in my tracks. "You will not!"

"Keep your voice down and keep walking! You didn't wanna take the Peterson's jeep so now we're stuck in this position. I warned ya this was gonna happen."

"Afternoon, gentlemen," Reese said, as we approached him. He reached out with an automatic handshake that Cody gripped firmly. "You guys look like you've been on the road awhile. You can wash up in the bathroom if you'd like. It's small and smelly, but the sink works."

"Haven't time," Cody said. "We gotta be on our way."

"Where'd y'all break down?" Reese asked.

"Just over the ridge," Cody said. "Around the other side of the mountain."

Reese pointed to a dented, blue Ford F150 pickup. "Hop in. We'll tow it back here and I can work on it first thing in the morning, getcha back on the road by nightfall."

"That ain't gonna work for us," Cody said. "You gotta fix it now. We need it ready to go."

Reese spit out his cigarette, dug his hand into his pocket, and withdrew a pack of Winstons. "Sorry guys, got my poker game at seven and seein' it's nearly five-thirty and I still gotta pick up your vehicle, take my wife to the store, and put the little ones to bed, I'm gonna be late as-is. But don't worry, I'll make sure you gotta place to stay the night. The Sumneytown Lodge always has a vacancy. They got nice rooms, too, cable TV and a heated pool."

Reese lit a cigarette. "You guys'll be on your way by noon tomorrow. And that's a promise."

Cody's mouth tightened, twitched, and then rose slightly at the corners.

"Guess that'll have to do, huh, buddy?"

He clapped my back so hard it almost knocked out my breath.

"By the way... uh, Reese, is it?" Cody said. "We might have a little trouble gettin' her out of the mud. Better bring a winch."

"There's one on the bumper."

Cody's eyes took on a twisted gleam. "Excellent."

He threw our bags into the truck bed, hopped inside the cab, locked the passenger door, and rolled down the window. I slid in through the driver's side. Reese got in and sandwiched me between the two of them.

"All right, Reese," Cody said, and rubbed his hands together briskly. "We're ready."

Reese fired the engine and pulled out of the station.

"Got any idea what's wrong with your vehicle?" Reese asked, as we turned off the main road and spearheaded up the mountain.

"Blown head gasket," Cody said. "We're certain."

"That'll require me to get up extra early to keep my promise. That is, if I got the parts. If not, I'll call Max's. His yard's got a bundle of old engines. I'm sure I can rig up something that'll get you where you're going. Course that might take another day."

The truck rounded a curve. The momentum pushed me hard against Cody. His .38 dug into my calf.

"Whatcha fella's names?" Reese asked.

"I'm Cody," Cody said. "And this here's Niles Goodman."

* * *

We drove along the gravel road. The Pathfinder was parked at an angle on the shoulder.

"Don't look to me like you's stuck in mud," Reese said.

Those were the last words to come out of his mouth before a bullet sprayed the meat off his face and onto the windshield. The boom of the gunshot rattled my ears. I jumped and hit my head on the roof.

"Ahhh!" I screamed, and lunged over Cody.

I had to get out of there. I had to get away from the mess. I fumbled to open the passenger side door, and then shoved Cody out so I could get out. I crouched to my knees, breathing deeply, desperately sucking in air.

"Why?" I screamed. "Why? Reese was helping us!"

"Listen you pansy-ass piece of shit! I had no choice! We had no choice! Once the Pathfinder got hooked onto that truck we'd be fucked!"

I bunched my hands into fists and banged them against my head. "This is too much! The guy had a family! A family! Where's your humanity? Your mercy?"

Cody stepped around and opened the driver's side door. He frisked Reese before the down-rush of blood reached Reese's pants pocket, pulled out the pack of Winstons, and lit one.

"This time," he spoke through the smoke. "There were no other options."

I knelt by the road, smelled the oily breath of the Ford's exhaust, blinked back tears.

"You've murdered six people!" I stated. "In cold blood! I can't believe this!"

He smiled absently. "You know nothin' about me. I've dismembered human bodies with circular saws. Run my hands through people's insides. For a man who's been properly frostproofed the landscape of remorse and morality is as obscure as the dark side of the moon."

I swallowed back my repugnance. What Cody was describing was a whole other level besides survival. I no longer feared him as a murderer but as an insane barbarian who would stop at nothing to get what he desired. A chemically imbalanced man. A psychopath who truly believed in his own preaching.

"You rationalize your actions," I said. "But you're still a killer!"

He grunted amusedly. "Do you think a lion feels bad when it kills a baby antelope to feed its young? Do you think the lion dwells on its violence as something bad, even though this hunting is necessary to maintain its own survival? Of course not! How can a person ever feel truly at ease if his morality is engaged in perpetual struggle over his true nature? Murder is nothin' more than a developed process of shuttin' off your societal conditionin' and revertin' to your natural, primal state. Bein' locked away in prison destroyed everythin' I had, everythin' I was. The way they treated me... how can I not hate the core being of civilized man and treat them as prey? Everyone who's a part of this culture is responsible for turnin' me into what I am. Society created the conditions for my metamorphosis."

"What about me?" I said, and got to my feet. "I'm part of this world, this society you hate so much. Do you blame me, too? Do you hate me?"

He pondered. Sweat glistened on his upper lip.

"Hate is defined as the desire to inflict injury," he responded. "And I wish none upon you, buddy. You knew me before prison. Before I developed the frostproof. I would never hurt you... unless, of course, you betrayed me."

He sniffed and spat, then pulled Reese's corpse from the truck smearing his own T-shirt with Reese's blood in the process. He dropped the body into the shallow drainage ditch beside the road.

"The frostproof is the realization that man is a wild animal meant to live free of restrictions. As humans conquer nature certain repercussions arise. It is inevitable that the strong among the population will become top-of-the food chain, like a shark is to the sea or a lion to the jungle. They're the ones who will rule this world and they'll need a leader, the top creature of the planet. With the money in Seattle I will begin a new reign; the era of the frostproof. It's time to fire the ovens and turn on the gas showers. The weak must be eliminated. Give me the tools and I'll cause genocide for the good of mankind."

He paused and raked his fingers through his hair.

"The natural state of Earth has always been a place for savages," he added. "Violence is innate, proven throughout our history in the thousands of wars humans have fought. We are a self-destructive race!"

He threw his cigarette, reached down, and dragged Reese into the shrubs.

I stood paralyzed with shock, afraid for everyone in the world.

* * *

Cool evening breezes dried the perspiration on my forehead. Cody hooked the winch to the Pathfinder's front bumper and then transferred the police radio and guns into Reese's truck. I got in the passenger's side careful not to brush my clothes against the smatterings of hemoglobin and human tissue stuck on the dashboard. Cody, unaffected by the mess, slid in, cranked the engine, and pulled out with the Pathfinder in tow.

We continued along the steep mountain terrain at a relatively even pace.

"All units in the general area," the police radio blared, after a long stretch of static. "Be on the lookout for a burgundy Nissan Pathfinder, license number MAJ291. This vehicle is in your vicinity right now. Extreme caution is warranted should any unit encounter the vehicle. Forward any information to Lieutenant Wayne McGovern of the Pennsylvania State Police."

"That McGovern motherfucker just won't give up," Cody said,

He slammed his foot on the brake and brought the truck to a near sliding halt in the middle of the road. He got out, walked around to the back, and unhooked the winch.

"What are you doing?" I asked.

"I'm gonna throw the officer's a twist. C'mon, help me push this."

"Push it where?"

"Where do you think?"

He pointed to the edge of the mountainside. It was a good 200 feet straight down.

"How are we gonna bust through the railing?" I asked.

Cody thought for a moment, then walked to the railing and kicked it hard. Aged wood splintered under his foot.

"That's how," he said, and broke an opening large enough for the Pathfinder.

He put it in neutral and we pushed from behind. Wheels spun quicker as we gained momentum and then let it continue on its own. Burgundy paint glimmered as the vehicle plummeted over the side of the cliff. A few seconds later, an explosion echoed through the mountains.

Cody stood in the middle of the road with his hands on hips as a whitish-gray balloon of smoke rose from the gorge. I watched the smoke ascend into the sky until the wind pulled it apart. Far to the west soundless lightning flickered against the coal bellies of storm clouds.

"Beautiful," he said. He sauntered over to Reese's truck and motioned for me to slip back into the passenger's seat. "We need another vehicle and fast. I don't know how much time we've got before the risk of drivin' around in this one outweighs its convenience."

He put the F150's transmission into gear and we headed off.

Chapter 11

Near Spokane, Washington
Sunday, April 26, 11:35 a.m.

Clouds thickened into wreathes around the mountaintops. Already in a state of great agitation, Cody grew frantic as spots of drizzle pockmarked the windshield.

I stared at the wipers playing tag and tried desperately to keep my thoughts on the here and now and off the images of Reese's burst face, the four dead police officers, or the fat sheriff we'd left lying in the roadway.

I didn't care about the drugs getting contaminated.

I didn't care about the shady alliances.

I didn't care about the money.

I just wanted to go home.

We traveled over the Rocky Mountains and stopped briefly at a summit to stretch and go to the bathroom. The view was expansive. From our height I could see the road twisting down the mountain and then straightening. In the far distance, a long, black band, six lanes wide sliced through the thick, piney landscape. Ground fog laid in the gullies like pools of cream.

"That's it!" Cody exclaimed. "Interstate 90! It goes for two hundred miles straight into Seattle. We fuckin' made it!"

"We're not there yet," I said.

He lit the last of Reese's cigarettes and crumpled the pack. A terrible, sinking feeling suddenly filled me.

"Three hours of highway drivin', that's all."

"Shouldn't we stay off the highway?" I said. "I'm sure there are back roads we— "

"No time!" A grimy lock of hair fell across his forehead. "The weather calls for a short break in the rain later today and then a second set of heavy downpours. I wanna get the stuff durin' that dry period."

"We should be cautious!" I stated. "Especially when we're this close to the city."

"How many fuckin' times do I have to tell ya, I don't wanna take a chance on the junk gettin' fucked up! The most important thing is to get to the heroin!"

"Police could be anywhere! Why take such a risk to save an hour or two? Why risk it all on impatience."

I spoke logically, but also out of my own consuming fear of us getting caught.

Cody dragged on the cigarette, tossed the filter out the window, and then turned to me with a frustrated look.

"All right," he said, and the truck slowed. "You made your point. You drive. Get on 90 and I'll figure an alternate way into the city."

* * *

Cody barked out directions as I navigated the twists and turns of the back roads to an on-ramp about sixty miles from where we'd been.

"We'll hit the highway from here," Cody said. "Otherwise these roads are goin' to take us way out of the way. There's plenty of traffic to blend in."

I conceded, merged, and had just sped to 55 mph when I glanced in the rearview mirror. My heart dropped into my gut. Flashing blue and red lights atop a police cruiser were dodging and weaving through vehicles and approaching us swiftly from behind.

"Fuck!" Cody glared out the back window. "Fuckin' cops!"

I wiped the flowing sweat from my brow. The squad car sped up and moved alongside us blaring its siren like a call to battle.

"I've fuckin' had it with this!" Cody hollered. "Stop the truck! It's frostproof time! It's frostproof time! It's time I did things my way!"

"I can't pull over! We'll never get out of this!"

"Do it!"

"I can't go to jail!"

"Stop the fuckin' truck!"

At that moment, the light drizzle exploded into a steady, lashing rain. Terrified, I flicked on the turn signal, slowed, and pulled onto the shoulder. The squad car followed and parked behind us.

Cody's lips pressed together so tight they turned white. "Do exactly as I say and do not interfere!"

"This is the Washington State Police!" a voice blared from a megaphone. "Remain in your vehicle and put your hands out the windows!"

My chest tightened. My body quaked. I was having trouble getting air into my lungs.

Cody sat as if in a meditative state, slowly, carefully, he unhooked the .38 from his ankle holster.

"No!" I whispered harshly.

"Hands where I can see them!" commanded the voice from the megaphone.

A police officer stepped from the squad car while his partner stayed inside. The officer approached my window slowly with his gun drawn. The officer's face look tense and determined. Rain dripped from the brim of his hat in long, stringy splatters.

"Get your hands out the window!" he warned Cody.

"What's the problem, officer?" Cody asked, and leaned toward my window.

"Hands where I can see them! This vehicle's been reported stolen!"

"Stolen?" Cody chuckled. "Impossible. My brother bought it from a lot three days ago. You've obviously made a mistake."

"Both of you step out of the vehicle and keep your hands where I can see them!"

"In this weather? You're jokin'?"

The officer targeted his gun on me. "Out of the vehicle now!"

"Fine!" Cody fumed. "We'll get out, but I want the name of the office that checks your…"

Like lightning, Cody pushed me over, lurched forward, and leveled his .38 inches from the officer's nose.

"Don't fuckin' move!" Cody snarled. "Don't sneeze! Don't cough! Don't blink! Drop your firecracker and put your hands behind your head."

The officer held his stance with his weapon at my face.

"Put the gun down, son," the officer said, his voice a blend of shaky terror and resilient bravery.

"Betcha I can pull my trigger faster than you can pull yours," Cody said. "Drop it or your life is done."

The officer hesitated.

"I mean it!" Cody stated. "You may kill my partner, but I'm gonna kill you."

The officer's gaze darted fearfully about the interior. His firearm slipped from his fingers and clanked to the asphalt.

A shot exploded by my right ear followed by the sound of smashed glass. For a second, I didn't know what had happened. Then I saw the holes in the cracked window and the frayed vinyl beside my shoulder.

Cody whipped his hand around and fired three quick shots through our back window, shattering what remained of the safety glass. The squad car's windshield exploded. The head of the officer inside whip-lashed and smacked against the dashboard. The officer by my window made a movement to run, but Cody quickly jerked the pistol back toward him and fired a shot by his head. The officer froze.

"Christ!" I muttered in a horrified voice.

Cody nudged me with his elbow.

"Get out."

He climbed out behind me, keeping the .38 steady on the officer. Passing traffic slowed and a few cars stopped. The occupants gaped at the scene. People were dialing their cell phones.

"Let's get down to business," Cody said. "I'm gonna teach you a lesson."

"What are you doing?" I shouted. "We've gotta get out of here! We've gotta run!"

"Stay outta this! It's frostproof time!"

Cody snatched his screwdriver with his free hand and plunged the tip into the officer's right eye. The officer screamed in agony and thrashed his arms. Shouts of horror and disbelief emitted from the stopped traffic crowded around us.

Cody caught the officer's head, steadied it, and jammed the screwdriver into the other eye. The officer yowled with pain. Cody started laughing, a high-pitched demented laugh. He thrust the screwdriver up and inside the officer's ribcage.

Lights sprang along the horizon, dozens of them; flashing blues and reds, coming this way from both directions.

My nerves exploded as I discerned the full extent of the approaching police armada. I took off running toward the tree line.

"Get back here!" Cody yelled.

I turned to see if he was following. He waved the .38 crazily toward the crowd of onlookers. People ducked down in their cars. Some screamed. He snatched his duffle bag and my gym bag and sprinted toward me.

He caught up amazingly fast, hurled me my bag, and we ran together into the forest.

Half a dozen police cruisers arrived, tires screeching. Officers leapt out and fired their guns, screaming for us to stop. Bullets whizzed overhead and smacked against trees and rocks with a slap-pop sound. We slid down a steep ravine into thick valley foliage and then clawed our way up a long, steep slope.

"We'll be fine," Cody said, panting exhaustively, his words coming out in frosty, white puffs. "We have the advantage of night. And the rain will mask our scents."

"What about helicopters?" I asked, exasperated. "And night vision? And infrared heat sensors? Did you think about those things?"

"The thick forest canopy will keep us camouflaged!"

"We're never gonna make it!"

"We will! Fear of the unknown is a cosmic insecurity we all experience. But there are ways outta any situation. We just gotta find 'em."

Chapter 12

Lost in the State of Washington
Monday, April 26, Time Unknown

We picked a remote and isolated path through the forest. Hour after hour we hiked over wild mountains, into virgin gullies, and through lush pastures and bucolic plains. Pillars of icy rain pounded on my shoulders and back. Insects relentlessly buzzed my head and bit my ears and neck.

Every few minutes, a helicopter swooshed unseen above the heavy blanket of fog and I'd flinch expecting a hail of gunfire to erupt from the sound. But the chopper would continue on its way and so would we, with dogs barking in the far distance.

"Toss the arm," I said, as we took a ten second rest on an overturned tree. "It's drawing scent."

Cody hunched over and hacked out a throatful of phlegm. "How many times I gotta tell you? It's necessary for the deal?"

“What good is the deal if you’re sitting in the electric chair!”

His eyes scoured my face. “We keep the arm!”

I spun around and hurled my gym bag deep into the shrubbery.

“You haven’t changed clothes since we left Pennsylvania,” Cody said. “Nothin’ in there is carryin’ scent.”

“I don’t care! It gives me hope!”

Cody walked about fifty feet in the opposite direction and withdrew the festering arm. He dumped the towel, ski masks, empty bottle of rubbing alcohol, and other contents, and spread them across the forest floor. He withdrew the neon-green sports watch and tossed it and the empty bag into the trees. Then he wrapped Jake’s arm in the soppy newspaper.

“This might draw and keep them here a while,” he said.

He strutted toward me with the rolled newspaper tucked securely under his arm.

“Shall we continue?” he asked.

And we trudged on.

* * *

The foul sky swirled with charcoal cones of merciless rain. Every few seconds, a bolt of lightning brightened the twisted branches of the forest canopy and I could see the next few feet ahead of me and move through the primordial darkness without tripping. Cody stopped periodically to bend over and suck in huge gulps of air, only to cough them out in raspy, choking fits.

"See how those left alive can turn into our biggest mistakes?" he said, during one of these brief rest periods. "The frostproof don't allow for compassion. Always pull the wings off the fly. Take away the bug's chances at getting away."

He sat on a boulder and pushed his wet hair behind his ears. Fatigue weighed on me. I sat beside him, bedraggled and spent. My bones ached. My cold, wet clothes stuck to my body like skin. Off in the distance, savage, uninterrupted barking merged with the rumbling sounds of oncoming storms.

Cody put his head back, stuck out his tongue, and tasted the precipitation.

"We'd better get movin'," he said.

I sniffed, wiped my nose with my sleeve, and squinted to see through the rain, mist, and foliage. "Which way?"

He dredged the map from his back pocket but it disintegrated into pulpy mush as he tried to unfold it. He mashed the paper into a ball and faced the dim, orange glow appearing in the east.

He pointed to the dark side of the horizon. "If I remember correctly, there's a road about nine or ten miles ahead that leads to an Indian reservation. We can use the frostproof to get a car there."

* * *

Rain eased but the clouds remained thick. We dropped into a creek to break our scents and trudged through knee-high water. The frigid current atrophied my calf and thigh muscles and I struggled to earn each yard.

All the while, police helicopters flew above the tree line and dogs continued to bark in the far distance.

Fear, worry, and exhaustion saturated every cell of my being. I was a shivering, broken mess.

Cody dredged his body up the muddy embankment and sat.

"That should throw off the dogs," he said.

I waded heavily to the shoreline and sloshed up beside him, my fingers blue with cold. A search helicopter roared overhead and we ducked under an outcropping of vegetation.

"Those choppers won't be flying much longer in this weather," he added.

I sat down, took off my waterlogged shoes, and wrung out my socks. My toes looked like white prune pits on the ends of my wrinkled feet. My teeth chattered.

"We gotta keep movin'!" he stated. "We gotta get the stuff."

My stomach asserted its desire for food with a shuddering rumble. I wrapped my arms around my belly and felt the xylophone of my newly protruding ribcage.

"You okay?" he asked.

"I'm just hungry," I replied. "That's all."

He studied me briefly.

"We could eat some of the arm," he said. "I mean, it's meat right? I'm sure Benny won't care if just a few bites are missin'. In fact, I'm so fuckin' hungry I think I'll have a bite right now. Want some? Make sure you gnaw around the map."

I watched, horrified, as he unwrapped the newspaper. Bacteria had devoured the dead flesh at an alarming rate and ivory bone protruded out the fingertips. The smell was a nasty fume.

"Mmmm," he growled. "This piece looks good."

He pulled the pinky finger all the way backward, popping ligaments and cartilage, then twisted the digit in a circle until tension finally ripped the skin. He raised the pinky finger to his lips. Spaghetti-like tendons dangled underneath.

Pre-nausea saliva flowed into my mouth.

He touched the tip of the finger to his tongue, held the finger there for a moment, and then tossed it into the woods.

He laughed. "Hadja fooled, didn't I? You actually thought I was gonna eat it, didn'tcha?"

I swallowed repeatedly and pulled on my damp socks and soaked shoes; it felt like slipping into sacks of icy mud.

"Relax, buddy, we're here," he said. "The reservation's just over this next hill."

"We haven't gone nine miles," I said. "Maybe three at most."

Cody rewrapped the arm in the soppy newspaper.

"Ever watch *Star Trek*?" he asked.

"What does that have to do with anything?"

"When I was in the psycho ward I watched a lot of *Star Trek*. It was the only thing on TV durin' my daily hour of television time. I developed quite an affinity for it. Saw every episode at least ten times. My favorite character was the engineer, Scotty. You wanna know why?"

I wiped rain from my eyes. "What's your point?"

"Scotty liked to fuck with captain Kirk's state of mind. Not directly, but he had his ways. I think he even enjoyed it. Scotty always overestimated the time it took to make repairs to the Enterprise, tellin' captain Kirk a repair to the ship would take three hours when in fact it would only take him an hour. Captain Kirk would then have two bonus hours he hadn't planned on."

Cody nestled Jake's arm back under his own arm. "I toldja it was nine or ten miles to the reservation when in fact it was about three. You mentally prepared yourself for a longer walk and spaced your energy accordingly. Now you have all this extra vigor to accomplish our next task. Whadaya think about that?"

I looked at him with squinted eyes. "I think you're crazy."

Chapter 13

Somewhere in the State of Washington
Tuesday, April 27, Time Unknown

The sun ascended and sliced an opening through the thick layer of cloud. It lit up the dripping forest and roused birds and insects into morning greetings. We continued a few hundred yards through thick Pacific Northwest foliage. Trees on either side of us thinned, and the steep slope flattened. We stepped onto a wide field with a dirt road passing through the middle.

"Welcome to the Spokane Indian reservation," Cody said.

He stared westward. "We're only about a hundred-twenty or so miles from Seattle. All things considered we've made pretty good time."

"What do we do now?" I asked.

He grinned and the right corner of his mouth twitched. "Wait for someone to come along… and then use the frostproof."

* * *

Sunlight felt warm and pleasant on my face. I sat in the dirt by the side of the road and watched rain puddles slowly soak into the ground and evaporate. Helicopters circled far to the north, but I no longer heard the dogs.

At some point, the rumble of a car's engine pulled me from my daze.

"Here comes our ride!" Cody exclaimed. "Make yourself scarce if you're not gonna help."

"There's no reason for excessive violence," I said. "Just tie the person's hands and feet. We only need the car for a few hours. He doesn't need to pay with his life."

Cody flashed me a steely smile. "I ain't got no rope."

I stood up from the mud and trotted into the bushes not wanting to be a part of whatever Cody was going to do, but knowing it had to be done if we were to survive. The faint mirage of a sedan came into view and shimmered on the horizon as dual opposites through the heat blur.

I crouched lower as Cody stood in the middle of the road. He was a dreadful sight, covered with dirt and blood, his hair a mess of leaves, twigs, and tangles. He smiled and put up his right hand. The car slowed and then skidded to a stop to avoid running him over.

"You crazy?" the driver yelled out the window. He was an old man with a russet complexion and long, straight, gray hair.

Without a hesitation, Cody walked around, opened the driver's side door, and aimed his .38.

The man's eyes widened. "What the… "

"Outta the car, Tonto," Cody said, and tossed the arm into the backseat. "I mean it! Right now!"

The man pulled his arthritic body from the vehicle and stood trembling with his arms above his head.

"I haven't any money," the man said.

"You got a cigarette?" Cody asked.

The man nodded, slowly lowered one arm, and fumbled with his shirt pocket. He withdrew a pack of Camel unfiltered. Cody grabbed the pack, pulled one out, and lit it. He sucked in a huge draw and filled his lungs with smoke.

"Ahhh," released in a gray cloud. Cody took another deep drag. "You just saved your life my Indian friend."

"Please," the man said. "I have children and— "

"Stop whinin', I just toldja I'm not gonna kill ya. Come on!" he yelled in my direction. "Let's get rollin'!"

I lifted the bottom of my shirt to cover my face and emerged from the woods.

"Sorry about this," I said, with as much dignity as I could muster.

"Just shut up and get in!" Cody said.

He raised the .38, leaned out the window, and blew a chunk out of the old man's leg. The noise caused a flock of crows to burst from a field. The man screamed, clutched his thigh, and collapsed.

"I didn't promise not to shoot ya," Cody said, and burst into sick, high-pitch laughter.

The old man lay writhing, whimpering in pain.

Cody waved goodbye and then stomped the gas pedal spraying the injured man with gravel.

I sat quietly in the passenger's seat, scratching at my scars, trying not to cry.

* * *

We pulled onto Interstate 90. Traffic multiplied. Rain started up again as the Scotch-colored water of Puget Sound came into view. Gulls soared chaotically on the stormy wind. Waves lapped against the shoreline. In the distance, an island ferry was nearly lost against the misty, fog-soaked background.

I had visited Seattle once before to attend a wedding and knew the basic outline of the streets. Cody turned up Second Avenue, onto Pike Street, and up Bellevue toward the Capitol Hill district.

Either I was getting used to the smell of the arm or else my own six-day dank odor oozing through the threads of my clothing masked the stench, because for a moment, I forgot we were still carrying it; until Cody reached around and planted the soppy mound of newspaper and flesh onto the console between us.

"Let's get the money now," I said. "So I can get out of here."

"First we're gonna see Benny and get ourselves cleaned up. We'll get the stuff later tonight."

"I thought we were in a hurry?"

"We've gotta see Benny first."

"Why?"

"Don't fuckin' argue with me!"

We crested a hill. In the valley below, the Seattle Space Needle poked up from the surrounding smaller buildings like an otherworldly monolith.

"This doesn't make sense," I said.

"It will," Cody replied. "It'll all fall into place."

* * *

The sun slid behind the Earth and the city descended into darkness and the oncoming thunderstorms. Cody drove up a steep side road and entered an ugly scar of a neighborhood. Boards pocked with bullet holes covered storefront windows. Garbage overflowed from street corner cans. Sidewalks were sparse, with a few souls braving the rain and huddling under awnings, drinking from bottles hidden within paper bags.

We made a few turns, barreled down a long street, turned again, and parked in an obscure, low-lit alley. We sat a moment and I listened to the rain strum steadily on the roof.

"Okay, buddy," Cody said. "We're on foot."

We got out and set forth at a brisk pace, passing graffiti-lined buildings and alleys populated by the homeless. We crossed another intersection and turned a corner. A block of narrow, crumbling row homes appeared. Streetlights glared against the dirty windows and created the unpleasant feeling of shadowy assailants waiting to pounce. Cody walked up to the door of an especially shoddy and neglected house and knocked three times in rapid succession.

Voices stirred.

I heard movement.

Cody knocked again, three times in rapid succession.

The door opened on a chain and a short, pencil-thin man with a helmet of frizzy brown hair and wearing a black patch over his left eye peered through the narrow space. His one glassy pupil blinked and his mouth curved into an awkward smile.

The door shut, the chain rattled, and the door reopened.

"Why goddam!" the man hooted. "Cody, you son-of-a-bitch! You made it! Shit, man, I'd been hearing all sorts of stuff aboutchu on the news. The press been sayin' you killed a lot of people. A lot... even for you. The FBI's slapped a title on you; the Highway Killer. Whadaya think of that? Shit, man! Goddam!"

Cody went inside without responding or introducing me. I fell in step behind him.

Benny's place smelled of decomposition and sweat; stale cigarettes and festering urine. Brownish-blue mildew stains blotted the wood-paneled walls. The floor was warped into bumps and valleys. Furniture consisted of a tired looking, brown-stained lime-green couch against one wall, and in the opposite corner, a scuffed coffee table with two bridge chairs. A thirteen-inch television sat cockeyed atop a plastic milk crate with *I Love Lucy* flickering soundlessly in black and white on the dusty screen.

"Hey, dude, how ya doin'?" The pencil-thin man extended a gangly hand in my direction. "Name's Edwin. Edwin Schloskiny."

I shook. It was like gripping a dry sack.

"You're the dude who rode with Cody, huh?" Edwin said. "Betcha that was fucked up, huh? Huh? Betcha it was."

I nodded and tried to push passed him.

"Sorry 'bout the pad," he continued. "Jake's problems forced us to rent a place fast. Shit, man, you should see the pad we got that's under surveillance! Nothing like— "

"You made it," an unseen voice interrupted from the next room. "Wasn't sure you would with the racket you've been causing."

Benny Harvin's rotund body emerged looking nothing like the arrogant college man of seven years previous. Eyes dark and lifeless sunk in a face full of deep fissures and lines. Long strands of greasy blond hair poked from his balding scalp and raked across his forehead.

"What happened out there?" Benny questioned. "What happened to keeping a low profile? I've been hearing stories of your escapades all over the goddam news."

Benny turned to me.

"Can't believe you survived?" he said, with disgust. "That's a fucking miracle."

"Hello, Benny," I replied casually. "It's been a long time."

He refocused on Cody.

"What the fuck were you doing?" he said, and poked his index finger into Cody's chest. "All those dead cops! Have you lost your mind? The point of your leaving was to distract attention from the stuff not turn you into the most wanted criminal in America! How are we supposed to conduct business with this kind of exposure? My people don't want to get involved in that! They're thinking of backing out because of— "

"Shut up!" Cody drew to his full height, squared his shoulders, and stepped to within a few inches of Benny's nose. "I did what I had to do to get back here. Business will be conducted as planned. I'm tired and hungry. What you're gonna do is make up two sleepin' areas, get us some dry clothes, and cook up some steaks, bloody rare!"

Benny's face flushed. He took a step backward.

"You got the arm?" he asked.

Cody unwrapped the newspaper and then heaved the arm at Benny's chest. It hit him squarely, splattering maggot-riddled goo across his white tank top. The stench of overflowing septic tanks filled into the room. My stomach twisted.

Benny examined the arm. "Why's the pinky missing?"

"We had a situation," Cody replied.

"Where's my duffle bag?"

"Sacrificed for the cause."

Benny fished out a mangled piece of paper from his front pocket, turned the arm palm-side up, and compared the rotted marks with the written matter. He smiled and tossed Jake's arm into a trashcan beside the milk crate.

"You're throwing it away?" I exclaimed. "After all it took to get it here?"

"We don't need it," Benny said. "The circle's complete. Though it did take longer than planned." He glared at Cody. "I didn't know he'd go to Philadelphia."

"Because I remembered you lived there," Cody said, turning his head to look at me. "What better cover than to drive with a guy who's never even gotten so much as a traffic ticket? It would have been a perfect route of travel had we not encountered that sobriety checkpoint. Your involvement in this whole thing is circumstantial, buddy. I hope you're not mad now that you know the truth."

"Truth?" I said, my anger rising. "What truth? You've been lying to me every mile of this trip! Your supposed parole! The distance to the reservation! Not harming anyone! Splitting the mon— "

I shut up.

Benny caught my mistake. "Splitting the money? Is that what you were gonna say? Is that what Cody promised you?" He stifled a laugh. "My dear friend, you are not getting half of anything. You're lucky we're giving you ten grand. And that was only agreed upon if you made it all the way here. If you'd quit, you'd have lost you life."

Cody bore the slightest hint of a smile and there was an unidentifiable glint in his eyes. "Sorry, buddy, I really needed the ride."

Fury nearly paralyzed me. My insides burned. My head felt dizzy.

"The hard part is over," Benny said. "The search for Jake has centered in California, for Cody in Oregon, and they've stopped surveillance on the area where we think the stash is buried. Basically, we're home free. We'll go early in the morning and get the stuff, you'll get your ten grand, and then you can be on your way home or wherever you wanna go."

"Let's get it now!" I stated. "We were in such a rush to get here."

"Early morning is safest," Cody said. "Benny's right, the hard part is over. Relish our success."

* * *

We cleaned up, put on fresh clothes, and filled our stomachs with steak. Afterward, Benny and Edwin snorted lines of cocaine in the kitchen while Cody twisted up a bomber of a joint and then sat down beside me on the couch. He offered me the joint and a lighter.

"No," I said.

"Ya sure? It's premium. How 'bout a beer? I know ya wanna beer."

My eyes caught his. "How could you lie to me about the money? I never betrayed you once during the trip."

"Some secrets are out," he replied, and squinted. "Some still remain."

He lit the joint and a grassy, vegetative odor overtook the rancid smells floating through the room.

"Benny set up a deal to sell the heroin tomorrow," he said. "We're meeting the guy in the early afternoon. It's up to you if ya wanna stay a few days or go."

"I'm outta here as soon as you put my share into my hand," I said.

He sucked the joint, held the smoke for a few seconds, and then exhaled.

"You might wanna stay around a bit longer," he spoke quietly. "I've still gotta few surprises." His mouth twitched. "I'm gonna get a few hours of sleep, I advise that you do the same."

* * *

Mold and fungus lived in the bathroom. It grew on the toilet, the sink, even on the planks of the Venetian blinds. My sleeping area was the grimy tile floor.

As I lay, I scratched at my scars and the wounds Kara had inflicted on my shoulders. I felt as dirty as the peeling wallpaper and shifted fitfully and uneasily; stared at the occasional headlight sweeping across the window; turned over in my mind the horror of the last few days. How I had been deceived and used.

Chapter 14

Benny's Apartment
Wednesday, April 28, 4:37 a.m.

Drowsiness settled over me. I lay there, neither fully aware nor unconscious, but in a shadowy cognizance of phantom scenarios and quasi-realities. The last few days spun in rewind and played over and over in my head. At some point, I must have fallen asleep because a hard shove to the shoulder roused me. Every neuron in my brain fired. I was instantly awake. My eyes popped open. Benny stood beside me looking down.

"Time to go'n get the stuff," he said, and stepped from the bathroom.

I scrambled up and glanced in the mirror. My eyes were swollen. Creases spread along my forehead. Several new strands of gray peppered my hair. I looked like I had aged five years.

A distant siren drifted in from the open window. I headed into the den. Cody was on the couch puffing on the charred bits of a cigarette. Flies were mating on the rim of the trashcan.

"I need a drink of water before we leave," I said.

Cody pointed toward the kitchen.

I crossed the den, entered, and flicked on the light. Fluorescent illumination flooded the room. I blinked as my eyes adjusted. Edwin sat at the table with a syringe sticking from his neck. Sweat pearled his forehead. His skin looked dull and waxen.

"Don't mind me," he said. "Just havin' breakfast."

I watched sickeningly as the tube filled with his blood and blended with an already present clear substance. His hand trembled slightly as he removed the needle, tapped the tube, and squirted a miniscule drop out the top. He re-inspected his neck with his fingers, poked the needle, and slowly injected the mixture back into a vein. He sighed out his nose and withdrew the needle leaving a small red puncture mark.

His one good eye glazed over and the lid swelled. He slid off the chair, banged his head against the floor, and came to rest beside the table leg, smiling as if he'd just experienced an explosive orgasm.

"ShitmanI'dshare," he mumbled. "Butthatwas the lastofit. Untilyouguys get back withthe realgoodstuff."

I looked away in disgust and wiped mouse droppings from the shelf. I grabbed a glass, cleaned out the grime with the bottom of my shirt, and filled it with tannic-colored liquid from the faucet.

Cody and Benny entered and nearly stumbled over Edwin.

"Look at that fuck," Cody said. "Can't even wait 'til the sun comes up before he sucks a needle."

He nudged Edwin with his foot. Edwin's head lolled to one side and he lost consciousness.

"You'd think he'd calm down after that infection rotted out his socket," Cody added. "Fuckin' junkie." He glanced in my direction. "Ya ready?"

I nodded and stepped over Edwin without so much as a concerned glance down.

* * *

Rain that had plagued us for the last several days drifted east and the sky washed clear. Moonlight flooded through the car windows and silvered the interior of Benny's '72 Dodge as we headed down the street.

"Looks like they found the car you came in," Benny said, as several police cruisers blew passed with sirens screaming. "Got the whole block cordoned off over there."

"Go a different way!" Cody stated. He slumped low in the car. "This ain't a fuckin' game!"

Benny made a sharp U-turn and we drove along Second Avenue toward the outskirts of the city.

"I'll bet the cross on Jake's wrist represents the old Temple Hill Mission." Benny said. "I know he made a bunch of deals there."

"I was thinkin' the same thing," Cody replied. "That'll be our first stop,"

We crossed a bridge, drove several miles north along Puget Sound, and then headed up a steep hill. At the top, we came upon a run-down brick cathedral with a large wood cross jutting from a crumbling slate roof. Above the door, a triangle-shaped stained glass window glowed prismatic in the early morning sunlight. The land was alive with greenery.

Cody leaned his head out the window and turned his face to catch the breeze. He sniffed deep.

"This is it," he said. "I can feel it."

Benny drove into the surrounding high grass and parked so the car was partially hidden. We exited and walked into the woods.

The terrain sloped down and squeezed into a forested valley. Cobbled throughout the undergrowth were large tufts of moss and wandering tree roots. Down the way and across a field, sunlight winked from a circular pond. Two trees stuck out like flagpoles on the far side of its otherwise bare, muddy shoreline.

"Okay, buddy," Cody said, an edge of excitement timbering his voice. "Wait here."

I hadn't time to state my objections before Benny took off running. Cody raced after him as if they were now competing for a prize. Benny quickly fell behind, panting like an overheated hippo.

"The dirt's been turned!" Cody yelled, as he reached the spot. "This is it!"

He dropped to his knees and clawed the loose earth. Benny caught up and bent over with his hands on his knees, gasping for breath. Cody reached down, pulled out a freezer bag, and showed it to Benny.

Benny smiled.

"It stayed dry!" Cody stated. "We're in business!"

He whipped the .38 from his ankle holster and held it steady at Benny's head. An expression of horror jumped onto Benny's face. His eyes broadened in disbelief.

"Bye, bye," Cody said.

"What— "

Bam!

The gunshot boomed across the expanse and echoed through the hillside. Blood flowed in a red gush from a hole in Benny's forehead. He stumbled backward, looked up at the sky, swayed, and then crumpled to the mud.

Waves of disbelief pulsed through my system.

Movement framed against a backdrop of pines, midway up the hill, and across the water, caught my attention. I ducked down behind a thicket of brambles and looked between the branches. Multiple blue-gray clad bodies descended through the trees toward Cody and where Benny's corpse lay.

"FBI! Don't move!" Several people yelled at once.

Half a dozen bodies surged from the forest and aimed firearms.

"Lieutenant!" an officer barked into a communication device. "Lieutenant! We got 'em!"

Cody looked fiercely from side to side. He dropped the bag, leveled his pistol, and fired. The officer talking into the communication device snapped up, shuddered, and then dropped over backward. Cody strafed the rest of the group until his gun clicked, then spun around and took off running into the woods. Shots exploded from the FBI's firearms as they swarmed after him, calling out to one another and yelling into communication devices.

"He's over here!"

"No! Over here!"

"Freeze!"

"There!"

Gunshots popped like firecrackers. A single FBI officer stooped beside his fallen comrade, checked his vitals, then picked him up over his shoulder and carried him away. Dozens more shots echoed through the valley in a fury lasting well over ten seconds. I heard shouts in the far distance but couldn't make out the words.

Then everything fell into silence.

An all-consuming muteness.

No bird chatter. No voices. No ammunition.

As if a mighty wind had barreled through and swept away the commotion. I stayed hidden; scanned the trees on the far side for movement.

Nothing.

A sudden, crazy thought hit.

The money was still in the ground!

* * *

All my life I'd played it safe, struggled because I was afraid of taking chances, suffered because I didn't have the guts to try something dangerous or new. Cody was right about one thing; everything worthwhile involved some sort of risk. Good fortune didn't just happen.

Saturated with sweat, I rushed down the hill, crossed the open area, and raced toward the far edge of the pond. My overworked lungs burned as I reached the two trees. Benny's bleeding body and the bag of heroin lay just a few feet from the hole.

I dropped to the ground and dug furiously into the dirt, shredding the skin on my fingertips and breaking a few nails. My hands felt something. I grabbed hold and pulled up a black trash bag about a quarter full.

I took off running, my body full of tremor and terror. Seconds felt like hours. I barely made it back to the edge of the woods before harried shouts announced the returning FBI. I hid behind a tree for a moment as their attention centered on Benny's body and the bag of heroin. I crawled slowly toward the thicker forest where the vegetation kept me well hidden.

I ran up the steep slope, breaking a new path, zigzagging, tearing through weeds and low-hanging branches until I collapsed into the high grass at the top of the ridge. I breathed great gasps of air and then ripped a small hole in the bag to peek inside. I nearly fainted. Thick bricks of hundred dollar bills lay at the bottom.

My body quaked from sheer fear and raw excitement. I could hardly believe it!

Sirens shrieked in the distance. I shook off my astonishment and waited for what seemed like an eternity, but it was probably more like a half an hour. When I felt certain it was safe, I snuck back to the Plymouth.

I ransacked the interior searching for anything that might aid me: a compass, a map, a shovel to rebury the money in a secret spot to retrieve later; nothing but old coffee cups and leftover bags of fast food takeout. I was about to abandon the vehicle when a glint of metal caught my eye. Benny had left the keys hanging in the ignition slot.

I jumped into the driver's seat, closed the door, and threw the trash bag onto the passenger's side. Sweat trickled from my armpits as I cranked the engine.

Vrrrr rrrrr

Nothing.

I smacked the steering wheel. "Come on!"

I steadied my nerves and turned the key again, my hands moving with mechanical slowness.

Vrrrr rrrrr rrrrr. Vrrrrr rrrrrr rrrrrr rrrrrr.

I kicked the gas pedal furiously as my heart punched my ribcage.

Vrrrr rrr rrr

"Start, you fucker!"

Vrrr rr vroom!

The engine growled to life. I shifted into drive and spun out of there.

I turned left, then right, and then left again. Nervous and disoriented, I tried to distance myself from the scene and was pleasantly surprised when I suddenly merged onto the highway and joined a sea of cars traveling into Seattle. I glided through lanes of traffic, turned down Sixth Avenue, and drove to a pricey, off-the-strip hotel that offered basement parking and the discretion I required.

In an almost dreamlike state of euphoria and disbelief, I nosed the car into a narrow, dimly lit space in the far back of the lot, and shut off the engine. I reached beside me, took a half dozen hundreds from the bag, and shoved the rest of the money under my seat.

A pistol dropped out from the springs. I picked it up. An 8mm heavy with a full clip.

Wonder if Benny had his own murderous plans for Cody and I?

I popped open the trunk and stashed the gun in the space where the spare tire should have been. Then I headed inside to guest registration.

* * *

Half an hour later, I had checked in under the name Nicholas Sebastian and was standing beside a king-size bed admiring the view along Fifth Avenue from six floors up. Cars filled the city streets below. Sidewalks teemed with pedestrians.

I grabbed several hundreds and went outside. I purchased a leather briefcase with a lock, a white oxford shirt, khaki pants and fresh underwear. When I returned to my room, I called the airlines to purchase a ticket to Philadelphia, but found it impossible without using a credit card.

I hung up, ordered room service, took a long, hot shower, and then dressed in fresh clothes. I took the clothes Benny had given me and threw them into the trash receptacle at the end of the hallway.

Then I called Samantha.

"Hello?" she answered.

"It's me!"

"Niles? Oh thank God! Thank God! Where are you? What are you doing? I'm totally freaking out! I've been freaking out for hours!"

"Why? What's wrong?"

"It's all over the news! Don't you know? Cody's been arrested in Seattle. They said his partner died! I've been so worried! I thought it was you!"

"What are you talking about?"

"He's a mass murderer! Cody's a mass murderer! He killed six police and they say he's responsible for dozens of crimes all over the country! They've been showing footage for the last hour! Turn on the news!"

I flipped on CNN. Sure enough, a scowling mug shot of Cody hung in the top corner of the screen, his face beaten, and the flesh around his left eye blue-brown and swollen shut. Pictures of the church meadow and pond flashed next.

"I've been cooped up in a hotel for two days," I lied. "Cody said to wait for his return and then he'd pay me."

The television switched to pictures of three FBI officers slinging a heavy stretcher covered with a white sheet. A photograph of Benny taken straight from our college yearbook popped up in the lower left hand corner.

"Niles, where are you?"

"I… I can't say."

"Why?"

"It's just better that you don't know."

"Don't keep me in the dark! How do I know you weren't involved? That you didn't harm anyone?"

"You think for a second that I'd do something like that?" I replied, and my brain produced brief images of the Petersons bound and gagged. "How could those thoughts cross your mind? I'm not involved in any crimes! None of this has anything to do with me! I'd be in jail right now if it did, right?"

"I don't know? I don't know where you are or what you've been doing or who you've been with! You could've been on a drinking binge!"

It suddenly dawned on me that alcohol and nicotine were completely free from my system and had been for days. Even the idea of getting drunk or having a cigarette seemed repulsive to me now.

"I don't drink anymore."

"I don't believe you! This whole thing is making me crazy! That man… that… that murderer, was in our home! I'm calling the police! They need to know!"

"They don't need to know anything!" I nearly shouted, and then I evened my voice. "Don't call anybody! Don't get involved! Cody's in custody and I'm okay. Everything's okay. That's what's important."

"We are involved! You were with him! Sooner or later someone is going to come around asking questions."

"No one is coming. No one knows about us. Calm down. I'll explain everything when I get home."

"When will you be home?"

"Soon."

"When?"

"Goodbye, I love you."

"Ni— "

I hung up the telephone and turned up the volume on the television. A newswoman was speaking:

"... and partner Benny Harvin, an associate of Jake Romano, who is still at large. Three officers were wounded in the shootout, one fatally. Harvin was killed. Larson now faces a multitude of charges ranging from kidnapping and assault to a string of murders and attempted murders.

Officials say Larson, the media-labeled Highway Killer, and Harvin may have been responsible for the deaths of as many as twenty-seven people in a cross-country killing spree that spanned eleven states in three weeks. Larson is also chief suspect in the death of Tom Donahue, a Montana security guard, and Washington University student Brenda Richards, believed to be one of the first victims in Larson's wave of brutal attacks. Leading the investigation is Lieutenant Wayne McGovern of the Pennsylvania State Police."

A tall, chiseled, man who looked to be in his mid-forties, neatly dressed in a pressed blue uniform, clean-shaven, with a touch of gray in his hair appeared on the screen.

"Good evening, Lieutenant," the newswoman said.

"Good evening."

"Can you tell us how you apprehended such an elusive and dangerous fugitive?"

McGovern straightened his shoulders. "Once these two were APB'd we had the cooperation of all counties. We knew Larson and Harvin were monitoring our communications through a stolen police radio so we fed them inconclusive information on our whereabouts. By enticing them to take certain routes and then following tips from their travels, we honed in on their position and drew a profile of where they might be going. Serial killers generally become more confident and daring over time, and when we discovered a smashed, burned-out Nissan Pathfinder containing weapons stolen from officers slain in Pennsylvania, and a shotgun from a slain officer outside New Castle, we knew we were getting close. We also received crucial information regarding their motives from a couple in Minnesota who narrowly survived a terrifying home invasion, though the woman did mention that Harvin was the more sympathetic of the two and appeared forced by Larson to participate."

A picture of the Peterson's front yard flashed onto the screen.

"In addition, two bags of Harvin and Larson's personal items were found in the woods a few hours outside Seattle along with a sports wristwatch that had belonged to Ms. Richards. We concluded that Seattle was their destination. It was just a matter of time before they slipped up and led us to their buried treasure."

"And reports say it was some treasure."

"Almost two million dollars worth of grade A heroin."

The newswoman turned toward the camera as if she were speaking directly to me. "That's some top-notch police work."

McGovern nodded. "This is an instance where Larson's own perceived brilliance became the catalyst to his downfall. His cocky overconfidence got him caught."

"Thanks Lieutenant and congratulations to you and your officers on a job well done."

The screen changed to a weather map of the Northwestern United States and another reporter broke in. "An unusual stretch of sunshine in the Pacific Northwest has Seattle farmers out and planting, but is it going to last? We have the all the wet details coming up after the break."

A sharp knock sounded at the door.

I switched off the television.

The knock repeated. An impatient double tap.

My heartbeat accelerated. I looked around for something that I could use as a weapon, anything that could injure a human being. I grabbed the table lamp.

"Who… who is it?" I asked, hesitantly.

"Room service."

* * *

I awoke from a deep sleep to the patter of rain against the windows. I got up and dressed, then took the briefcase and went down to the car to pack the money and 8mm. I drove a few streets over and parked the Plymouth in a far, unobtrusive corner of a shopping center parking lot.

I got out with the briefcase and stood for a moment looking at the sky before heading back to the hotel.

I sighed. The nightmare was over. I looked down at my scarred hands, my hairless arms, the smooth, almost silky skin where my fingerprints used to be… and knew the police would never come.

* * *

"Good morning, sir," the clerk greeted, as I approached the hotel's front desk. He was an older gentleman with a neatly trimmed beard and silver hair. "How may I help you?"

"I'm checking out. Sebastian, room 847."

The clerk typed on his keyboard.

"Okay, Mr. Sebastian, here we are. Your bill with room service and long distance telephone call comes to one hundred and fifty-five dollars exactly. Will this be cash or charge?"

"Cash." I handed him two one hundreds. "And I'd like to overnight this briefcase. Does the hotel provide a packing and mailing service?"

"We do."

The clerk handed back three twenties, a ten and a five. I slipped the money back into his hand.

"Make certain that it arrives at its destination tomorrow morning."

The clerk smiled and palmed the bills. "Yes, sir."

"And could you call me a cab?"

* * *

I bought an airline ticket with cash.

Recollections of the horror-filled week bubbled in my head during the six-hour flight home. I wanted to tell Samantha what I went through, that I'd witnessed tremendous evil that would blemish my soul for the remainder of my life. I needed to unload this emotional baggage and somehow attempt a return to normal.

But I couldn't say a word to her. All I could tell her was that I was cooped up in a hotel room watching television while waiting for Cody top do his business and return. And guess what? Now we're rich because of it.

I yawned, looked around at the half-empty airplane cabin and then out the window at the sparse, twinkling lights of United States suburbia 35,000 feet below. The glittering galaxy of a city stretched endlessly ahead.

Chapter 15

Philadelphia, Pennsylvania
Thursday, April 29, 8:57 p.m.

Darker more ominous thoughts skewered my mind during the long cab ride from the airport to home.

Could I ever erase the images of those dead police officers? Could I really keep this much money a secret from the law? Would Cody or the Sumneytown ranger eventually reveal my identity or ID me somehow?

"You can let me out here," I said, to the driver and pointed to a mini mart.

I didn't want him to know where I lived.

The driver pulled into the parking lot and I got out. I paid the fare, tipped him twenty dollars, watched him pull away, and then headed down the street toward home. High above, the moon was bloated and radiant.

I approached my driveway. The yard was a tangle of weeds and unattended grass; we hadn't the money to fix the mower. Through the milky haze of the porch light, I saw the front of the house in dire need of maintenance and paint. I sighed, walked to the door, and guided the key into the lock.

"I'm home!" I announced, as I stepped inside.

I expected to see a canvas and paints set up in the living room, Samantha hunched over numerous jars of color, Oliver barking joyfully and bounding toward me.

Nothing.

The house rested in an eerie stillness.

I stepped into the kitchen. On the refrigerator was a piece of paper informing me that Samantha had taken Oliver and gone to her mother's for the night. She needed time alone to think.

I sat down on the couch and switched on the television. Exhaustion weighed heavily and the screen quickly became a blur. My eyelids slid shut.

"Cody Larson... "

My eyes popped open. On the screen was a woman reporter and the rebroadcast of the 11:00 o'clock news. I looked at the time on the wall clock. 2:07 a.m.

"... will be charged in the death of prominent Minnesota doctor Norman J. Peterson, who died yesterday of injuries inflicted by Larson before his capture. Dubbed the Highway Killer, Larson, who for the past three weeks held the country hostage with his exploits, is charged so far with an unbelievable twenty-eight counts of murder, sixty-seven separate kidnapping and assault charges, and three cases of fraud. He will be indicted today as investigators try and piece together his bizarre path of carnage."

The screen flicked to a pre-recorded interview of Lieutenant McGovern. "Larson is a brutal psychopath who chose his victims at random, killing without hesitation or remorse, seeing others merely in terms of how he might use them to fulfill his own needs and desires."

The screen dissolved back to the female news anchor. "Larson is currently being held without bail in the Seattle City Jail. He has vehemently opposed the insanity plea requested by his— "

I shut off the television, laid back against the cushions, and closed my eyes.

Fell into an astral lagoon of dreams.

Chapter 16

Home

Friday, April 30, 12:47 p.m.

It was past noon when I awoke. The mailed briefcase was on the front porch. I unwrapped the packing and put two stacks of money into the top kitchen cabinet, and then put the 8mm and the briefcase with the rest of the money in the shed under a bunch of old boxes and rags. I secured the shed with a combination lock.

After a quick lunch, I poured a cup of coffee and went upstairs to the bedroom. I cleaned the shelf of Seagrams and Budweiser bottles, threw away the Nicorette gum, and then sat down at my computer.

I stared at the waterfall screensaver.

I thought about everything Cody had put me through.

I needed to purge my conscience.

I needed to unload.

I started to write a story.

* * *

Samantha's red Ford Tempo pulled up our driveway. I ran down the steps and greeted her as she opened the front door. Oliver leapt at me, tongue lolling and eyes gleaming. I gave him an obligatory ear scratch as he raced in circles at my feet.

"You've lost weight," Samantha said, matter-of-factly. "And you're face is all scratched up."

I swept her into my arms, kissed her, and turned her around. To me, she was the sweetest sight in the world.

"What's wrong with you?" She unhooked and pushed me away. "Where's your car?"

I put my index finger over her lips, took her hand, and escorted her down the hallway into the kitchen. Oliver followed tail wagging.

"What's wrong with you?" she asked, again.

She stood by the sink and looked out the window. I stepped up to her, bumped my cheek against hers, and kissed the tip of her nose.

"Enough already," she said. "How do expect me to react to all this? You disappear for a week with a serial killer and then show up acting as if our whole world and relationship is renewed. I'm still mad at you."

"I have something to show you."

She crossed her arms. "What?"

Her sight followed my hand as I reached into the cabinet and took down the stacks of hundred-dollar bills.

Her eyes widened. She blinked and grasped the back of a chair.

"What is that?" she gasped.

"Cash," I replied. "This is why I had to leave so quickly and couldn't tell you why. It was all about the money. It was all about paying off our bills and providing you a better life. That's why I went with him." I dropped the bricks onto the table. "This will change our lives."

Her free hand trembled as she reached out and picked up a bundle.

"How much?" she asked.

"About a hundred grand."

She dropped the wad and brushed her hands together as if she'd just held dirt.

"I feel sick. We can't keep this."

"We can!"

"Where do you think Cody got it? From the pockets of the people he's killed! This is blood money! This is wrong!"

"It's not Cody's money!" I stated. "It's not from his victims! This money's been sitting in the ground for so long it's like found treasure. I knew you wouldn't approve, but I also knew what the money could do for us. I was a chauffeur, nothing more. I swear! The money belonged to a drug dealer who died!"

"Did you know this drug dealer?"

I hesitated. "Yes… but that was a long time ago. He wasn't a friend."

"Did Cody kill him?"

"No."

"Who did?"

"It's not important."

"Not important! Have you lost your mind? This is dead drug dealer's money! We have to return it!"

I picked up a stack, tore off the rubber band, and spread the bills across the kitchen table. "There's no one to return it to."

"Then we'll give it to the police!"

"And they'll ask questions! And then we'll be involved in something we don't want to be involved with."

"Someone will find out! Keeping this money will become a curse!"

"Impossible! No one knows about it, no one's looking for it, and no one's missing it. We can spend it, we can donate it, or we can burn it in the fireplace. The only thing we can't do is give it back. It's up to you. I got this money for you! It's yours to do with as you please."

She crossed her arms. Stood that way a moment and stared at the bills.

"I guess..." she said finally, and bit her lower lip. "I mean... it certainly would help."

I reached around, put my hands on her shoulders, and gazed into her eyes. The corners of her mouth lifted with the fleeting traces of a smile.

"Trust me, baby, our problems are over."

Chapter 17

JUNE

Spring greened into summer, insurance paid for the "stolen" Sentra, and the nightmare week gradually faded from the foreground of my thoughts.

Samantha and I each leased a new car and we had an extension built onto the back porch with a quaint, one-room office at the end for me. We also had a small ornamental pond dredged at the far edge of the property. I placed a bench there so I could sit at dusk and listen to the crickets and tree frogs. It gave me peace.

Samantha seemed genuinely happy and my constant, sober presence quelled her worries that I would sink into my addictions and apathy. She seemed jubilant over our bank account and my newfound joy: writing a novel.

She got pregnant.

I bought a watertight container and buried the remainder of the cash under the bench. I didn't want Samantha to know how much we really had. Not until Cody was locked away for life and the police had completely closed the investigation. I also purchase a small Beretta handgun, which I kept behind the old holiday silverware in the kitchen cabinet's second drawer. Paranoia still held a tight grasp on my psyche and I didn't want to be in the house defenseless.

I stored the 8mm behind a box of old magazines in the shed.

Chapter 18

Thursday, June 28, 11:45 a.m.

Storms had been brewing all day and now a gray tarp of cloud hung over the house. Thunder rumbled and peas of rain drummed on the roof. It was a perfect day for staying inside and finishing my book.

Oliver suddenly let out a string of vicious barks that ended with a high-pitched yelp. I'd never heard him make such sounds before and I cut my attention from the novel and leaned back in my pneumatic chair.

"Oliver!" I called. "C'mere, boy!"

Lightning flashed.

Movement caught my eye. Something hidden in the shadows of the deck.

A person?

Cody's hulky figure moved through the doorway into the office.

I jumped from my chair as if he were a figment of my imagination; a villain from a nightmare. His head had been shaved and his cobra tattoo looked animated and alive.

"What the..." I shouted.

"Hey, buddy," he replied.

"How? How is this possible?"

His left hand was jammed into a gun-swollen pocket and his right pinched a cigarette.

"Haven'tcha heard?" he replied.

Dark glasses fell to the tip of his nose and he stared above them with an evil glare. I shook my head, feeling each muscle in my neck tighten with terror.

"The Highway Killer has flown the coop," he said. "Claimin' more victims." He spoke sprightly, like a news reporter doing a human-interest story. "Gloria Peterson, alleged nurse and beloved wife of the late doctor Norman was found hacked to pieces in her home early yesterday mornin' with her children gutted beside her. Whoever committed this crime must've been really pissed off at her for squealing to the cops."

Blood in my veins turned to ice.

He winked. "Also caught up with that ranger who took us into town. He was easy to kill. Never even saw me coming at him with the knife."

My stomach turned. My throat tightened. I spun around to rush from the office, but Cody came quickly across the room and blocked my path.

"Going somewhere?"

He flicked his cigarette against the wall. Tiny red meteors of hot ash dropped to the new carpet.

"Ain't you curious how I escaped? Dontcha' wanna know how I, Cody Larson, the evil genius, outwitted the country's best and brightest police officers? Let me tell ya. Those dumb fucks put me into a cell directly above the laundry facilities. Guess they didn't know condensation softens concrete, especially around the exhaust vents. How's that Beatles song go? Oh yeah. I got a diggin' device with a little help from a friend," he sang. "Killed two guards with a little help from a friend. Stole a laundry truck with a little help from a friend, with a little help from a frieennnnd."

Edwin emerged, dripping from the rain. He wore a black trench coat over filthy jeans and a white T-shirt.

"Hello, Niles," he said, and smacked his lips in an air kiss. "Shit, man, I can't tell you how good it is to see you again."

Cody looked around. "You're doing quite well for yourself since the last time I visited. New addition to the house. New car in the driveway. New landscaping. Nice new deck."

"What do you want?"

He pulled a screwdriver from his ankle band and poked his index finger into the tip. "I wanna know what the fuck happened to my money."

"You came all this way for that?" I faked a little laugh; it didn't sound convincing. "I don't have it!"

"I ain't a fool!" Cody stated. "The cops searched the hole! The heroin was reported on the news, but not the cash. That's very peculiar, don'tcha think?"

"How could I possibly have gotten the money?" I said. "Cop's were everywhere. It was chaos."

He shrugged. "You tell me. Benny certainly didn't steal it."

"You're mad!"

He turned in Edwin's direction. "Show him your new toy."

Edwin pulled an Uzi submachine gun from underneath his jacket and pointed the barrel at me.

"Let's make this very clear," Cody said. "I'm not leavin' without the money, so at this point ya better pray you can come up with it or ya got some rich friends who can lend it to ya."

Edwin escorted me at gunpoint from my office, across the deck, and through the kitchen back door. Oliver lay unmoving by his food dish surrounded by an oval puddle of blood.

"You bastard!" I spun around to punch Cody.

Edwin jammed the Uzi's stock into my stomach sending me to my knees.

"Damn animal wouldn't shut up," Cody said. "Look, I told you I'm not fuckin' around! Now where's that purty wife of yours?"

I stared over at Oliver, my heart aching, my fury rising.

"I don't know," I replied through clenched teeth, though I knew she'd be home from the gynecologist soon.

Cody faced Edwin. "He's lying. There's a note on their refrigerator calendar about an appointment. Go to the end of the driveway and wait for her."

"She won't be home until tomorrow," I said quickly.

Cody looked at me, clicked his tongue, and shook his head. "Remember the rules of the frostproof, buddy. Edwin go!"

"Shit man," Edwin groused. "You know I hate the rain."

"You live in Seattle, the wettest city in the nation!"

"I don't choose to live there," Edwin muttered. "It's where the best heroin is."

"Get the fuck outside!" Cody's turned his attention on me. "We'll be discussing the whereabouts of my money."

"Our money," Edwin corrected.

Cody glared at him. "Our money. Now get out there!"

Edwin slouched toward the door. Cody pulled two chairs from the kitchen table. He withdrew a pistol from his pocket and waggled it at me.

"Sit down," he said.

I went for the chair.

"Slowly," he grunted. He ran the gun-sight up and down the length of me. "We can do this easy or with a lot of mess."

I repositioned the chair and gravitated closer to the cabinet's middle drawer, where I kept the Berretta. My nerves wound tight but I concentrated on remaining calm and focused.

"I don't have the money!" I reiterated.

Cody tapped the pistol against the table and then put it down as if tempting me to try and take it. He folded his hands. "I don't believe you. We'll know the truth once your wife gets— "

I jumped up, threw open the drawer, and caught the Beretta's grip. Cody sat, completely unfazed as I aimed the small barrel at his chest.

"What the fuck is that?" he questioned. "A squirt gun?"

He chuckled but it was a humorless sound.

"It'll do the job!" I stated.

Our gazes remained locked for an uncanny few seconds. I froze, didn't know what to do.

"Go ahead, buddy," he cooed. "Shoot me. Go ahead, shoot me! Shoot me dead!"

The gun shook in my hand.

Quick as lightning, Cody grabbed his pistol and fired to my left. Plates stacked on the shelf blew apart. He fired to my right, shattering the stove's heat-resistant glass.

"Go ahead!" he screamed. "Shoot me! Shoot me dead!"

I bolted toward the kitchen door and slammed my body against the wood. The handle busted loose and I flew onto the deck into the railing. I clutched the Beretta and took off running down the sloped lawn.

Heavy rain distorted my view. Edwin shouted from the head of the driveway, asking what was happening. I raced around the property and dove into a soppy drainage ditch along the perimeter of the woods.

My breath burned in my throat. My mind scrambled with activity. I had to keep Samantha from coming down the driveway. I had to warn her. Lacquered with mud, I crawled from the ditch and scanned my surroundings. Cody and Edwin stood beneath the overhang looking the other way, oblivious to my position, their voices drowned by the rain.

In the distance, the purr of Samantha's high-performance BMW engine drew closer. I sprinted through the woods toward the road. The barrier of shrubbery had become thick and lush, fueled by unusually heavy spring rains. It slowed me down. Sticks and weeds tore at my legs, but no pain registered. I charged from the brush.

The purr turned into a roar as the BMW passed. I stood in the middle of the road screaming and waving my arms, trying desperately to get her attention.

A hundred yards up ahead, she turned into our driveway.

* * *

Rain subsided. I navigated through the woods to the Mini-Mart, picked up the outside payphone, and called Samantha's cell phone collect.

"Hello?" she answered in a weak croak.

"Sam, it's me!"

"Niles," she sobbed. "They killed Oliver!"

She shrieked and a dull thud came over the line.

"Hey, buddy," Cody greeted with a low, sinister growl. "That was a clever idea but greatly flawed. After all we'd been through I knew you wouldn't have the guts to fire. Now, get yourself together, throw that firecracker into the woods, and come on back inside. We have a lot to discuss and we're not gonna chase after you in this weather."

Samantha wailed another terrified scream. My ears curled.

"He's pointing a gun at me!" Samantha screamed in the background. "Oh God, Niles!"

I inhaled a deep, steady breath, tried to not let fear or anger cloud my judgment. "Okay! All right! I'll be there soon."

"Now we're gettin' somewhere!" A noticeable exhilaration took over his voice.

"Give me your word that you won't harm Samantha," I said.

"Of course, but I do need an incentive for you to act quickly." His voice turned stoic. "You have ten minutes, not one second more. Oh, and if I haven't mentioned it yet, congratulations on becomin' a daddy."

A click snapped in my ear and the line hummed.

I slammed down the receiver.

I scrambled through the woods back toward the house. I needed more firepower than the Beretta. I had to get the 8mm from the shed. To get to the shed, I'd have to sneak along the side of the house. As I neared my property, my eyes picked up objects out of the rainy gloom. Two forms stood inside by the living room window in full view of the lawn.

To get to the house was a wide-open thirty-foot dash.

* * *

A long roll of thunder preceded the approach of another thunderstorm. Precious minutes were disappearing. Finally, the silhouettes by the window moved out of sight. I sucked a deep breath, jumped up, and sprinted.

I was completely focused, intent on making it to the shed. My ears half expected to hear shouts and the sound of gunfire while my nerves readied for the sudden, sharp, searing pain of a bullet.

Neither came as I reached the wall by the kitchen. I pressed against the aluminum siding and slid to the corner of the house. From there, an overgrown row of arborvitae blocked the scene from the living room window.

The back kitchen door opened.

I froze.

"I know you're around here somewhere," I heard Cody say, his voice raised to carry over the property. "Ya got three minutes! You hear me? Three minutes!"

He went back inside. Rain exploded in a furious downpour and continued in a steady drain.

I crept around to the front, craned my neck, and looked into the den window. Samantha was on the couch, trembling and chewing on her knuckle. Her face was pale, her eyes tear-streaked and frightened. Her paintings were in shreds and piled in front of her. Oliver's bloodied body lay in the middle of the canvases.

Cody stood a few feet from her with his back to window. Edwin was sitting Indian-style on the floor eating the sandwich I'd made for my lunch. The Uzi rested across his lap. The wall clock showed 2:55 PM.

I hurried along the house to the shed, unlocked it, grabbed the 8mm, and inserted a full clip. I also grabbed some string.

The sprint back to the woods was risky, and again, I anticipated shouts, the sound of gunfire, and piercing pain. Neither came. I dove to the ground at the tree line and crawled along the woods to the bench beside the pond.

I pulled up a chunk of grass and buried the 8mm on top of the watertight container, careful not to clog the barrel with mud. I shoved the Beretta into my sock, tied it loosely with the string, and headed toward the house; stomach quivering, my muscles lit with popping nerves.

Chapter 19

Even at a distance, I could make out Cody's face pressed against the living room window, watching as I trudged up the hill toward the house. His image disappeared and a moment later, the front door swung open.

"Get inside!" he ordered.

I stepped in. Rainwater dripped from my clothing and formed an instant puddle at my feet. He patted me for weapons, but stopped at my knees. My heart nearly skipped.

He ushered me toward the living room. Samantha eyes flashed to mine, pleading; like Gloria Peterson's, and the woman who burned in the minivan.

"Niles," she said, in a weak, shaky voice. "Give him whatever he wants."

"You should listen to your wife," Cody said. "Where's my money?"

I looked him straight in the eye. "You think I'd bring it with me? It's the only leverage I have."

"You have no leverage!"

Cody swung his pistol in Samantha's direction and fired three shots I into the couch. Fabric beside her exploded, spewing foam like popcorn. She screamed, curled her legs in a fetal position and hugged her womb.

Edwin emerged from the kitchen, Uzi in hand. "What's all the ruckus?"

"We've wasted too much time with this shit!" Cody stated. "Go get the money now or your lady's dead!" He snatched the Uzi from Edwin's grip. "Edwin, keep an eye on him."

"Shit, man, what are you doin'?" Edwin responded. "I need that."

Cody released the safety. "He won't try nothin' while his lady's with me."

Edwin started to say something but Cody's finger pointed in the direction of the door.

"Get going!" he commanded.

"My needle first? C'mon, man, you promised! I'm jonesed!"

"When ya get back!"

Edwin bristled and turned to me. "This is all your fault! I hope you get what's comin' to ya!"

I looked once more at Samantha sitting terrified on the couch, her hands balled into fists, her eyes wide and tear-filled, her bottom lip trembling.

We headed out the door.

* * *

Rain fell like pebbles. We tromped down the back lawn, leaving deep, muddy footprints in the newly germinated grass.

"What are you doing?" Edwin asked, as I stopped beside the bench. "You're supposed to be gettin' the cash."

"The money's here," I said. "Buried."

"Shit, man, you expect me to believe you've buried all those bucks under a bench? Whadaya think I am, some dumb ass off the street? If this is a trick your lady's gonna get her head blown off."

"Exactly," I said. "So why would I lie?"

Edwin pondered that fact for a moment and then rubbed his chin. "Well… shit, man, get digging then! I ain't gonna get my hands dirty."

I crouched and pushed my fingers into the saturated earth.

"See?" I said, and lifted a handful of mud. Edwin moved behind my right shoulder. "The soil's still loose from when I dug the hole."

"Yeah, well, hurry up! I'm jones'n for my needle."

I repositioned my feet, adjusted my balance, and reached down.

"Okay," I said. "Got it."

Edwin leaned closer.

I pulled the 8mm from the earth, swung my elbow, and smashed it into Edwin's abdomen. He stumbled backward gasping for air. I came at him fiercely and pummeled the pistol squarely at his jaw sending him reeling into the mud.

"Shit, man!" he cried and clutched at his face as blood streamed from his mouth. "You broke my teeth!" He spit chunks of enamel. "You broke my teeth!"

I pointed the 8mm at his chest. "Get up!"

"My teeth! My fuckin' teeth!"

I kicked him hard in the side.

"Get up!"

"Ohhhhh, my teeth," he moaned.

I kicked him again.

"Up!"

"Stop! Stop! Okay! Okay! I'll get up!"

Edwin struggled to his feet in obvious pain. His lower lip had ballooned to three times its normal size. Bright red lines of blood seeped down his chin. I aimed the 8mm at his head.

"Don't move!"

"That's... that's Benny's gun!" he sobbed. "How'd you get that?"

I reached into the hole with my free hand, keeping the 8mm steady on him, and pulled up the watertight container.

"What's that?"

"Start walking!" I ordered.

"Is that the money?" His eyes widened despite his obvious hurt. "You really got it!"

"Walk!"

He let out a snide little chuckle as we headed toward the house. "That money ain't gonna help your cause. You're dead and so's your wife!"

"Shut up!"

"You understand what I'm sayin'? You're life's over. Cody doesn't care about trade-off's. He ain't gonna make any deal with you."

"I said shut up!"

"Don't you get it? Cody's cleanin' up his past. Gettin' rid of those who knew him before his transformation. He believes he can rule the world; kill the weak and strengthen the strain of humanity. He's a madman who thinks he's a messiah. He ain't gonna negotiate."

The front door swung open. Cody stood behind Samantha, one hand clasped on her shoulder, the other pressing the Uzi's barrel into the small of her back. An unlit cigarette hung from his lips.

"Both of you disappoint me," he said, as the cigarette bounced in his mouth. "We could have done this so easily. Just a nice little exchange. Now it's gonna end messy."

I struggled to maintain my composure.

"We can talk this through," I said. "We can end this without anyone getting hurt. You know you can trust me to keep our secrets."

"My trust in you is dead," he grumbled, and waggled the barrel at the watertight container. "Is that my money?"

I looked at Samantha and then looked away. "Yes… it's all here but a hundred and fifty grand. There's twenty more in our checking and forty-five in our savings accounts. Plus another ten in a mutual fund. You can have it all."

Samantha's face took on a look of incredulity.

"I knew you had it!" Cody exclaimed. "I knew it the whole time!"

"I'll go to the bank and make the necessary withdrawals," I added. "But I want your word that you'll leave us alone."

A huge crocodile smile overspread Cody's face. "How many seconds do ya think I'd have to hold the trigger before the bullets cut your wife in half?" he asked. He glared at Edwin. "And Edwin, I can't believe you fucked up again. How many times is this gonna happen before I gotta get rid of you?" He turned back to me. "I'm tellin' ya, buddy, it's hard to find a good accomplice these days, too bad you didn't work out." He shook his head and clucked his tongue. "It's a real shame neither of you worked out."

The weight of my weapon suddenly felt very heavy. My arm muscles began to give. It was becoming harder to keep the gun steady against Edwin's ribcage.

"That's Benny's piece," Cody said, as he noticed what type of gun I held in my quivering hand. "How'd ya get that? Careful, it packs quite a wallop."

Cody backed up slowly with Samantha in tow. I followed them into the kitchen keeping Edwin as my hostage and placed the watertight container onto the table.

"Take the money," I said. "Let her go."

"Just like that?" Cody emitted an obnoxious laugh. "Ya know, buddy, the whole time we were together I couldn't figure out why ya didn't kill me. Leave my body at the side of the road and go your way. No one would have ever known. Then I remembered college. You hangin' out in our dorm room preachin' the virtues of peace and love and listening to that Grateful Dead hippie bullshit music. I realized no matter what the circumstance, you're too much of a moral pacifist to ever take the shot. You have no frostproof in ya. You're one of the weak. A lamb among the masses. You don't deserve a place in my new order." He squared his shoulders. "You can't shoot me, you can't shoot Edwin, you can't shoot anybody. This charade is over!"

My stomach knotted. I suddenly realized in a blinding flash of insight and horror that I had made the ultimate miscalculation. Cody didn't need Edwin anymore, just like he didn't need me once we'd reached Seattle. He didn't care about the money in the bank. He cared about the satisfaction of knowing he was right that I had taken it. I was bargaining with useless tools. I had no chance. I was going to lose this confrontation. I had to do something! I had to do it now!

Cody released his grip on Samantha, pushed her aside, and stepped up to the kitchen table. He looked at Edwin, shrugged, and said simply; "You suck."

Explosive hammering filled the room. A track of bullets popped across Edwin's stomach. Innards flew out his back and splattered against the wall. Pain stabbed into my side. Samantha screamed.

I hunched down and felt my own warm blood traveling through my fingers and down my thigh. A second burst of bullets slammed into Edwin's skull and whizzed passed my ears.

"Run!" I shouted to Samantha. "Take the container and run!"

She snatched it and bolted out the kitchen toward the front door.

Cody fired chaotically. Holes peppered the walls and windows. Splinters of glass and wood bounced through the air. I dropped to my knees and scrambled toward the back kitchen door. He let loose another burst. Sulfur-scented gun smoke filled the kitchen. Plaster chips flicked off the walls and hit my face. The back door fragmented and burst off its hinges.

The barrage stopped and I heard the click of a reload.

I hopped up, took two fat steps, and leapt through the splintery frame and over the porch. I landed hard in the mud. The 8mm flew from my hand. I raised my head and saw Samantha huddled behind a lilac bush.

"What are you doing? Get out of here!" I screamed, as I scrambled toward her direction.

She stared at me with horrified eyes, her hair matted and tangled from precipitation and pieces of vegetation.

"I… I couldn't leave you!" she sobbed.

"C'mon!"

I gripped her arm, took the watertight container, and pulled her across the yard toward the woods. Rain pounded mercilessly on our backs. I turned my head and saw Cody standing in the doorframe with the Uzi's muzzle engulfed in white, turbulent, flames of expulsion. A maelstrom of noise preceded a hailstorm of bullets. They tore through branches and shaved off the tops of shrubbery. I grabbed Samantha's shoulders and drew her down.

"Keep going!" I urged, weakened by pain and blood loss. I held the container tight against my chest. "He wants the money! Not you! Go! Go!"

Bullets snapped across our last position and exploded in the mud with hard powerful pops.

"No," she said dazedly. "We go together."

"I'll slow you down!"

"I don't care!"

She reached out her hand and I took it. We ran, muddy, breathless, and terrified, toward the road.

* * *

A jackhammer of automatic gunfire clipped the rocks beside us. Samantha stumbled and slid head first into a trench. I slid down the mud beside her and hunched over her protectively. The bottom had become a temporary river of rushing floodwater.

Lightning forked overhead followed by a long roll of thunder.

Cody's dripping figure appeared on the ridge above us. The corner of his mouth twitched spastically.

"This is the price you pay for not havin' the brains to outwit me!" he shouted, over the sounds of the storm. "Stealin' my money was the first big chance ya ever took and were completely unprepared to deal with the consequences of your actions! Hand me the money without a fuss." He aimed the Uzi at Samantha. "And I'll make her death less painful."

Staring up at Cody, his insanity and madness shining like a thousand burning suns, it suddenly became clear what I had to do; what I must do; what it was going to take to keep us alive.

"You want the money?" I stated. "Come get it!"

I grabbed the container, unscrewed the top, and flipped it upside down, spilling bricks of cash into the rushing water. Paper bills began washing downstream.

"You fucker!" he shouted.

My eyes focused completely on him as he lowered the Uzi slightly and leaned forward to step down. Quick as a rocket, I snatched the Beretta from my ankle and aimed steady at his chest.

His eyes widened. His mouth dropped.

Sound muted.

Time seemed to slow down.

My emotions detached and disintegrated. Fear. Hate. Love. Remorse. Compassion.

All gone.

I was an empty shell.

Then I felt the beginnings of the frostproof trickle into my cells and take over my senses. A pure, dark presence of unadulterated evil and dispassionate emotion. Energy born from the deepest depth of congenital instinct and pure animalistic survival. I suddenly saw Cody as nothing more than bug that needed swatting; a mess that needed cleaning; a thorny impedance upon the silky sands of my smooth life.

I pulled the trigger.

Bam!

A bright red circle popped just left of Cody's sternum. The Uzi dropped from his fingers and he fell forward without a peep, toppling down the embankment, landing twisted and broken a few feet from Samantha and the raging water's edge. She hid her face in her hands.

"You... " he gurgled, and coughed up a mouthful of blood.

He made a final galvanic effort to reach for the Uzi as bubbles of snot and blood dribbled from his nostrils. He rolled onto his back, gasping for air.

"You pulled the wings… " he wheezed, and the muscles in his face relaxed. His eyes clouded over. "Off the fly."

Air drained from his lungs. His eyelids slid halfway down and then stopped. His pupils fixed.

Samantha lowered her hands. Ropes of wet hair pressed against her shoulders.

"Is he dead?" she asked, in a barely audible whisper.

I stared at Cody's fallen form, unable to rouse in myself any guilt, shame, or regret; unable to feel any emotion at all.

I nodded mutely.

She buried her head into my right shoulder. I put my arms around her, the pain of my wound forgotten.

"I love you," she sobbed. "I love you so much."

I kissed her muddy forehead. Felt the frostproof begin to dissipate from my system. Felt my emotions slowly returning.

Felt myself getting back to normal.

* * *

Day had drained into night by the time the police paperwork had been inked with details and they'd packed Cody and Edwin into body bags. Samantha went to stay with her parents; the forensics units had finished cleaning; and I found myself alone in the house, pacing, and fully awake. My bandaged side ached (the bullet had gone straight through missing vital organs) and my nicked-up arms and legs itched, but the police didn't consider me a suspect of any crimes so I was free to do as I pleased.

I stared at the multitude of quarter-sized bullet holes riddled about the walls of my house, each pock encircled with orange chalk. Plywood covered the kitchen doorway. Yellow caution tape strapped the room.

I sat down on the gray canvas chair to watch the eleven o'clock news. We, of course, were the lead story. I turned up the volume.

"It's an incredible end to the saga of Highway Killer, Cody Larson, when Chalfont County resident Niles Goodman fatally shot the fugitive in the woods outside his country home.

Goodman, a former college roommate of the serial killer, told police that Larson had stopped by seeking refuge from the masses of FBI on his trail. When Goodman refused to aid the murderer, he says Larson went on a rampage, killing his own partner, wanted drug felon Edwin Schloskiny, and then spraying the house with bullets.

Goodman told police he grabbed a pistol from Schloskiny and escaped with his wife into the surrounding forest where the fatal confrontation occurred. Goodman, who said he's just a normal guy that was forced into protecting his wife, has earned the respect of police units across the country and will be honored on Friday by Lieutenant Wayne McGovern of the Pennsylvania State Police."

She looked into a different camera. "In other news, two people were found stabbed outside Manyunk earlier today in what police describe as a possible copy-cat— "

I shut off the television, stepped to the window, and gazed into the black acreage of night. Standing alone in the house, I felt different, aged, changed in ways no language can explain or describe.

I went into my office, grabbed a pen and a tablet of paper, and wrote the final chapter of my book.

Epilogue

Notes from Niles Goodman's Personal Journal

There are nights, long, sleepless nights, when I can still hear Norman Peterson's labored breathing. I can picture each dead body in my mind, smell Jake's arm, and see the shock in Cody's eyes right before I shot him dead. Memories of those awful days are forever seared into my consciousness.

Although things have quieted some since my first fiction novel, *Frostproof* reached number seven on *The New York Times* bestseller list and the movie rights were sold, I still sometimes wonder if anyone will ever find out it was I who rode across the country with the notorious Highway Killer instead of long-deceased Benny Harvin.

What a shock to my fans that revelation would be.

There are moments when nightmares of the FBI descending upon my beachfront property are as vivid and haunting as that day in Seattle and I have to remind myself those possibilities are gone, fragments of a past effectively erased.

I eventually recovered $473,000 of the money I'd dumped into the stream, which I donated anonymously to the Peterson children and the families of Cody's victims. The rest of the cash that washed away... who knows? But those first couple of months after the incident the local economy did seem to prosper.

Some time later, while sitting in a dentist's office waiting to have a cavity filled, I happened to pick up a complimentary copy of *Field and Stream* magazine. Tucked away in the back pages was a small article on the Creekside Inn. It seems U.S. Marshalls had raided the place on a tip from a lost group of college road-trippers and the bodies of two men, fugitives from a prison escape down south, were discovered packed in the ice chest. They found Kara with her head in the oven and the gas turned on.

These days I'm pretty busy writing my latest novel and doing promotion for the old one, although I still enjoy the occasional lap around the pool and taking long, solitary walks among the dunes with my German shepherd, Chance, as company.

My despondence and self-destructive ways are long behind me, replaced by the complacency of a loving wife, a daughter, and a son. My attempt back then to provide Samantha with a better life proved to be an incredibly dangerous and reckless act, and the course of our destinies has been significantly and forever altered because of the experience.

She still can't believe how much things have changed and every so often asks me again to tell her what really happened during that horrific week with Cody.

I always reply the same; "It's all in my book. Name's and places have been changed but everything that happened is right there on the page."